Dirty Deeds

A Salt Mine Novel

Joseph Browning   Suzi Yee

Text Copyright © 2024 by Joseph Browning and Suzi Yee

Published by Expeditious Retreat Press
Cover by J Caleb Design
Edited by Elizabeth VanZwoll

For information regarding Joseph Browning and Suzi Yee:

Subscribe to their mailing list at their website: https://www.joseph-browning.com.

Joseph on Twitter: https://twitter.com/Joseph_Browning. Joseph on Facebook: https://www.facebook.com/joseph.browning.52. Suzi on Facebook: https://www.facebook.com/SuziYeeAuthor/.

By Joseph Browning and Suzi Yee

THE SALT MINE NOVELS

1. Money Hungry
2. Feeding Frenzy
3. Ground Rules
4. Mirror Mirror
5. Bottom Line
6. Whip Smart
7. Rest Assured
8. Hen Pecked
9. Brain Drain
10. Bone Dry
11. Vicious Circle
12. High Horse
13. Fair Game
14. Double Dutch
15. Dark Matter
16. Silent Night
17. Deep Sleep
18. Home Grown
19. Better Half
20. Mortal Coil
21. Import Export
22. Numbers Game
23. Dirty Deeds
24. Going Under
25. Second Wind
26. Uncanny Valley
27. Ice Breaker
28. Love Lost

Chapter One

Moscow, Russia
4th of March, 4:15 p.m. (GMT+3)

Major General Alexander Petrovich Lukin stared out of his seventh-floor window onto Lubyanka Square. Ten centimeters of snow had fallen last night—just enough to completely cover the uninspired cobblestones. From his vantage point, it looked no different than any of the thousands of fields outside of the city, and the soft white veneer allowed him to pretend there was productive earth underneath. Even the piles abutting the roads left by snowplows had a fresh coat draped over them, hiding the grit, dirt, and black carbon spewed from passing automobiles. His eye had been drawn to it throughout the day. It was almost beautiful, and as long as he wasn't subject to the elements, he preferred it this way—cold, crisp, and clean. Each time he peered out, he'd expected something to sully the picturesque landscape, but the pristine lacquer held, much like his recent turn of good fortune.

His chairmanship of the Ivory Tower had had a bumpy start after the botched delivery of the phoenix egg to the general secretary of the Chinese Communist Party, and his subsequent ill-treatment by Zhao Sheng, head of the 88th Bureau of the Ministry of State Security of China, had left a sour taste in his mouth. However, when one of his agents recovered the same egg in Duncith, it had been Sheng's turn to eat crow: although a week late, the new chairman had delivered the goods. Perhaps he wasn't as incompetent as they'd initially thought. The status that came with maintaining international relations was not without fiscal reward, to the tune of one million USD. He'd known being chairman would have its perks, but he'd never imagined they would come with so many zeros.

Then, in December, he'd waged his first battle against the Interior Council. The issue was the Salt Mine's presence in Duncith, and he'd used the newly discovered Myrskyvaris to leverage his proposal to permanently embed a triad of experienced field agents in the eld Magh Meall city. It had been hard fought, but eventually all nine members came to his side: they couldn't let the Mine have the upper hand in the area if they wanted to continue their special arrangement with China. His plan had been approved in full in early January, and the search for the right agents was ongoing.

As good as all that had been for his ego, his first significant addition to the Ivory Tower's property portfolio had earned him the most cachet: a fully-modernized Italian villa in Portoferraio on Elba Island. The snow in Lubyanka Square might look beautiful today, but it wasn't remotely in the same league as the Tyrrhenian Sea. He'd already planned two weeks of working vacation there, and the extended Roman dock on the property would serve as a haven for more than one mega yacht during his stay. At last, word was getting around: Major General Lukin was a man to know.

You'll never finish your work if you keep daydreaming, his inner voice scolded him and he reluctantly brought his attention back to his desk. In many ways, running the Ivory Tower was like being a general in a war. He had to create strategic goals and have opinions regarding the tactics involved, but he had to rely on his subordinates to carry them out. Unfortunately, those subordinates were inherited from his predecessors and the ghosts of those prior generals hovered over everything. It had taken him months to familiarize himself with all of the Tower's operations, and he'd finally gotten to the point where he could divest himself of personnel he would never have chosen in the first place and fill their newly vacated positions with those he favored.

His first such substitution was Konstantin Dmitriyevich Oborin, the agent responsible for recovering the phoenix egg. Despite the loss of one of his triad members, Oborin persevered and got the mission done. That was the kind of person he wanted leading his ranks. Lukin was so pleased with him, he'd even considered a small fiscal gift after the Chinese had paid him before he remembered the unspoken rule of Russia: money went up, not down. Promoting Oborin was a suitable reward because it would put him in a better position to extort those beneath him, but an actual payout was positively un-Russian. The great pruning continued as he freshly signed off on the latest batch of staff changes, certain that the Tower would come out a much-healthier tree on the other side.

Next, he turned his attention to the various financial markets around the world. In addition to operational matters, he tended to the financial wellbeing of the Ivory Tower, much like a CEO of an investment company. It had been substantially easier to take a firm hand after Volsky's disappearance—all he had to do was follow the money. Given how rife the corruption had been under his predecessor, it hadn't been hard to wet his beak while showing improvements in performance to the Interior Council.

He performed his due diligence by checking each of his major holdings. Once he'd confirmed everything was as expected, he began shutting down his office for the weekend. The concept of the weekend was a luxury he didn't have as a field agent but was part and parcel with office life. He had to be available by phone should something happen, of course, but he was no longer the one who had to execute orders. *Leave it to the young ones; I did my time*, he reminded himself whenever he felt the itch for action.

"Goodbye, Starshina Monkey. Have a good weekend and don't do anything I wouldn't do," he bid the framed bits of crackled paint sitting on his desk. The scowl of the grizzled capuchin monkey smoking a cigar did not change, but he imagined his longtime confidant smirked and replied that that didn't leave much out, considering Lukin's plans.

He jumped into the armored Land Rover Defender that served as the chairman's vehicle and pointed it north toward the dacha. He'd assumed it belonged to Volsky—the pompous ass had certainly made it seem that way—but it was actually a *gosdacha*, a state-owned property. Yet another perk of the position. The chairman of the Ivory Tower driving himself was a break from normal protocol, but Lukin was an exceptional driver and the only time he didn't want to be the one behind the wheel was when he was inebriated or busy with work or pleasure.

The dacha was a few miles outside of Moscow, on a private lake lined with a handful of the most exclusive names in all of Russia. All of the properties around the lake were accessible via a single looping road that was protected from casual access by a fortified guard station manned by none other than the Russian Army itself: a statement of the value of the property and the people within. It was always occupied by two soldiers that freely brandished their AK-103s as a deterrent to casual inquiries. They immediately recognized the Tower's Land Rover and Lukin barely had to wait for the retractable bollards to descend into the ground before continuing his journey. The soldiers smartly saluted him as he passed.

The dacha was built in the 1930s, but of the original structures only the boathouse had survived. The main building had been torn down and completely rebuilt at the turn of the century and the lovingly carved Russian gingerbread-and-lace ornamentation was the only physical reminder of what the original dacha had looked like. It was modest by today's oligarchical standards, but it was still exceedingly luxurious: six bedrooms, an indoor pool, and an entertainment room with oversized theater seating. It was all at his disposal after Volsky disappeared…although he suspected his predecessor was "disappeared": paid the full and final price for his failure at Bratsk. Lukin quickly binned any obvious personal touches Volsky had made—the man had had no sense of taste—but had yet to completely redecorate himself. He'd been far too busy with work, and only found time to hang up an enlarged giclée replica of Starshina Monkey on the wall of the living room. That monkey had seen him through his darkest years and it deserved the dacha experience as well.

Lukin headed straight for the *banya,* which would take time to come to temperature: a toasty 70°C with 50% humidity. As it warmed up, he unpacked his things and undressed, dousing himself with cold water before entering the aching heat. He stayed for ten minutes and stepped out for another cold shower before going back into the steam. The stark contrast was just what he needed. He repeated the process over and over, sweating away the stress and cumulative weight imposed on him by his position. He would never admit it out loud, but being chairman wasn't as easy as it looked.

When he emerged feeling fully human, he took a shower in tepid water and donned a plush bathrobe for a clean shave with a straight razor. Halfway through his left cheek, he remembered something he'd forgotten to do before he left the office. *You couldn't have thought of that before I went into the banya?!* he cursed at his brain as he finished shaving. Fortunately, it didn't involve going back to the Lubyanka building, and he always brought his laptop with him in case work beckoned. A simple email to the right subordinate would suffice, but the task seemed offensive and distasteful, like having to take a shit right after showering.

He felt some of the stress creep back into his muscles as he tapped away and felt the pull of work—there was always more to do—but he pushed back. In twenty minutes, his driver would arrive to chauffeur him to a night out. He would have a wonderful meal at an exclusive restaurant in Moscow, followed by some clubbing with two lovely young women he'd hired for the night. He didn't have to pay for company—he was still an attractive, fit man, albeit of a certain age, and his newly acquired position and wealth certainly didn't hurt—but well-paid escorts gave him what he wanted without question or complication. More importantly, they would do whatever he asked when they eventually ended up his king-sized bed, and the same couldn't be said of a mistress, girlfriend, or wife. With those mental images firmly set in his mind, he shut his laptop. He had finally reached the top of his profession and it was time for him to start playing as hard as he worked.

He walked to the bedroom where he'd hung up his clothes for tonight before taking his steam bath. In a shadowy corner, a man dressed in a thick jacket, his pants tucked into his boots, was waiting for him. In his right hand was a Makarov PB with an attached suppressor pointed directly at Lukin.

It took Lukin a split second to recognize the man from his days as an agent. "You!" he cried out as he propelled the full force of his will against the intruder, but the man was prepared for it and metaphysically swatted it away. He said nothing; they both knew why he was here and Lukin was owed a bullet. He fired a single shot that passed through Lukin's head and left destruction in its wake. Only then did he come closer, putting two more suppressed shots into Lukin's heart.

When he finally spoke, it came out with a snarl. "*Requiem in Inferno.*"

Chapter Two

Moscow, Russia
5th of March, 3:07 a.m. (GMT+3)

Nikolay Yastrzhembsky soared through the air, riding a thermal on his flight south before winter's arrival. He determined that he was a solitary bird of prey because he was not surrounded by a flock and his eyes kept scanning the ground for a meal. Perhaps he could narrow it down if he made a kill: hawks, eagles, and kites struck with talons while falcons used their beaks. He saw promising movement below just as he heard his mobile phone ring. His avian self flew faster to try to escape the modern sound that did not belong to the natural world, but his mind was trained to respond. He instantly remembered who he was: a major general of the Russian military and the general secretary of the Ivory Tower's Interior Council. If he was being called at night, it was for a good reason.

Shostakovich's four-tone DSCH motif repeated as his aerial adventure came to an end. He softly slid out of bed, palmed his phone, walked into the hall, and closed the door behind him. It was a well-practiced maneuver to avoid disturbing his wife, even though she'd become inured to late night calls on state business. She rarely roused with the worry and panic that'd struck her when both of them were younger people. He sometimes wondered how much of that was aided by the sleeping pills she'd started taking in her 40s.

"Yes?" he answered tersely. If it was an erroneous dial, it would not reveal who they had called and anyone looking for him would expect nothing more.

"Sorry to bother you so early, Major General Yastrzhembsky, but we have a situation," the voice on the other end greeted him.

The new kid, Yastrzhembsky quickly identified the caller and dredged up a name to go with the doughy young face that flashed in his mind's eye. "Dimitri, I told you before not to say that, no? Of course, we have a situation. Why else would you be calling at this hour?"

"Yes, of course, General Secretary," Dimitri Kissov apologized. He'd become one of Yastrzhembsky's personal assistants two months ago and was still learning the Major General's preferences. There were a lot of them.

Yastrzhembsky sighed at the future of Russia. "Just tell me what's happened; no need to preface it. I know it's important. It's always important."

"Yes, sir," Kissov replied automatically, and Yastrzhembsky could tell how bad the news was by the pregnant pause. "Chairman Lukin has been murdered, sir."

Yastrzhembsky brushed aside any lingering drowsiness or annoyance and became laser focused. "What is known?"

"He was killed in his dacha by occult means. Military police found him shortly before 2:00 am along with the body of his driver. We've since taken over."

Yastrzhembsky walked downstairs to the kitchen as Kissov reported the facts. "Who's our agent in charge?" he queried as he loaded the coffee machine in the dark. It was an old habit he'd picked up early and never abandoned: when it's dark outside, keep the interior dark as well to make a sniper's job more difficult.

"Spassky's in charge. With him are Proskuriakova and Alexandrov."

Yastrzhembsky bobbed his head. "Good. He shouldn't fuck it up. Tell Spassky to keep the scene as pristine as possible. I want to look at it myself before they start investigating."

"Yes, sir. Shall I arrange transportation?"

"No. I'll take care of it," Yastrzhembsky declined firmly. It was nothing against Kissov, but caution seemed prudent. If Lukin's death was part of a larger plot that also included replacing him, it would be unwise to let others be privy to his precise movements. "Just tell them to wait. I shouldn't be long."

With his order issued, Yastrzhembsky hung up and made a call to a trusted driver, one that would be indifferent to the hour. He slipped a cup under the spout and started the brew but didn't wait for it to finish. It would be easier to down after it had cooled.

He went back upstairs to his home office and into the en suite bathroom he used when his duties came at off hours. The sink was lined with a duplicate of his toiletries and it looked downright bare without the various scrubs, creams, and serums his wife used in her beauty regimen. His eyes automatically sought out offending flecks of gray and white in the mirror. It wasn't so much for vanity's sake as survival: a full head of dark hair projected vitality in a profession that valued strength. When he'd started dying his hair, he hadn't considered the end game—that it would eventually stop conveying gravitas and make him the butt of jokes, like a bald man with a cheap toupee. *At least all the hair on my head is mine*, he thought proudly.

He took to his ablutions with a disciplined economy before changing out of his pajamas. He forewent his normal suit and tie; he was going into the field. The idea was both exhilarating and daunting. He may have started out as a soldier, but he'd long ago clawed and charmed his way out of the trenches and into leadership. For decades, he'd sent out pawns to be his eyes and ears on the ground and do all the dirty work that was required.

Lukin had been one such chess piece until he'd proven himself capable of more—one of the few elite field agents the Tower possessed who Yastrzhembsky considered as well-trained as a Salt Mine agent. More ambitious than politically adroit, his ascension to chairmanship was largely propelled by Yastrzhembsky once Volsky's failure was too great to ignore. *And now he is dead.* Reiterating it made it sink in a little more, and the elimination of an asset for whom he'd invested so much personal collateral summoned a sense of loss that hadn't naturally arisen.

He gave himself the once-over in the full-length mirror and saw a late middle-aged man of average height and build dressed for the outdoors—the appearance of someone spending a weekend at their dacha. He reflexively sucked in his stomach and pulled his shoulders back to present the most flattering reflection. While he'd staved off the weight gain that normally came with aging and a less physically demanding job, he was no longer the lean killing machine he'd been in his youth. There were no prominent love handles, but under his clothes was an undeniable softness overtop his abdominal muscles.

He methodically armed himself and concealed everything before going downstairs. His coffee was now cool enough to drink quickly and the jolt of caffeine was just what he needed. He left the empty cup in the sink—a signal to his wife that he'd been called away during the night—before meeting his driver.

Once they were on the road, his mind began to speculate. He couldn't help but wonder if Lukin's assassination had been at the behest of another Interior Council member. They knew he was Yastrzhembsky's pet; they all had pets of their own that they constantly jockeyed into preferred positions. With Lukin dead, the great kingmaker game would start all over again in earnest. The motive and method were plausible enough, but the timing seemed rushed and unusually heavy-handed for the Interior Council. They were a calculated bunch that concocted subtle schemes in the scope of years, not months. The start of Lukin's chairmanship had had its bumps, but he'd come through when it counted and all the Interior Council seemed satisfied, if not pleased, with his performance thus far.

Enemy action was another option. Taking out the chairman of the Ivory Tower was certainly a decisive blow. He mentally ran down the list of governments and magical organizations that stood to gain from hamstringing the Tower, but he ran into the same problem with each one: why use magic? It was much easier to use a bullet or a bomb to take out a practitioner, particularly one of Lukin's caliber. Munitions didn't carry karmic costs nor did they leave any of the magical traces that could be occultly tracked and identified. In an arcane world, they were far more anonymous.

Of course, it could be a bottom-up conflict within the Tower: one of Lukin's subordinates displeased with their current situation, who thought beheading the hydra may make it grow a new head more favorable to them. This was the possibility that worried Yastrzhembsky the most; outright internecine fighting was a recipe for institutional disaster and had to be nipped in the bud post haste. It would explain how they got to

Lukin in the heart of Tower territory, and suggested complicity or malfeasance in the *Komitet Magicheskoy Bezopasnosti*. The KMB was the part of the Tower that worked solely within Russia to control and contain the use of magic to sanctioned parties and for sanctioned purposes. No one within the Ivory Tower would gun for Lukin without thinking they had an iron-clad way of getting away with it.

Yastrzhembsky grunted as he ruminated. All he had were questions and half-baked theories, but one thing was certain: whoever was behind the death needed to be publicly punished—not the general public, but the private circle of practitioners public—and severely so. Such an attack against the Ivory Tower could not go unanswered. If the murderer could not be found, he would eventually decide upon someone to pin the entire affair on, someone he wanted to get rid of. He wasn't one to waste the opportunity of a crisis.

The advantage of a frame-up was that even if the actual perpetrator initially got away, it wouldn't *look* like they had, and that was far more important than justice for Lukin's death. Chairmen came and went, but the Ivory Tower persisted. The real killer would happily keep their silence and if they were also Yastrzhembsky's enemy, they would tip their hand in some other way. He'd weathered many squabbles and coups in his tenure and with Lukin's demise, he would be on high alert.

As the vehicle rolled along, Yastrzhembsky started making a short list of those whose absence would make his life better.

It seemed more fruitful than conjecturing on the unknown and it certainly improved his mood.

Chapter Three

Moscow Outskirts, Russia
5th of March, 6:03 a.m. (GMT+3)

The sun still languished beneath the horizon when Yastrzhembsky's armored SUV arrived at the gate of the dacha community. The bollards were up to prevent vehicular traffic from passing through, and there were now four guards on duty instead of the typical pair. Such was the reality of security: never enough when it was needed and too much after something bad had already happened. They stopped his car gruffly, but their demeanor changed once he identified himself. Even their salutes were somehow obsequious.

"I want to speak to the guards who found the body," Yastrzhembsky stated.

"Junior Sergeant Michurin and Corporal Gmelin are waiting for you in the guard station, sir," the lieutenant in charge answered and directed the driver toward a single-story building of reinforced concrete faced with rough stone to make it appear less martial and more decorative to those who visited the dachas. The inside was a single room with a small area walled off for a toilet and shower. Two unarmed men were sitting at a table while a third brandishing an AK-103 stood at the door.

Yastrzhembsky surmised many things at first glance. The two seated soldiers were the ones who had found Lukin. Based on their shell-shocked expressions, whatever waited for him there was harrowing. The two men were not magicians but the guard at the door was, which suggested Spassky had quickly locked down the scene and isolated them from the others before they could share what they had seen.

"I will speak with them now," Yastrzhembsky paused before adding, "alone." Even though he was in plainclothes, he conducted himself in the manner befitting his rank. The guard responded in kind, leaving his post to the major general and closing the door behind him as he left. Yastrzhembsky drummed up his will and coated himself with it, adding an arcane boost to his naturally intimidating presence. "Names and ranks," he crisply commanded.

His voice snapped them out of their fugue. They were bolstered by Yastrzhembsky's spell and the balm of routine— something familiar and automatic that didn't require them to think, just act. They took to their feet, came to attention, and complied.

Yastrzhembsky directed his focus to the higher-ranking one. "Tell me what happened. Leave nothing out."

Junior Sergeant Michurin cleared his throat. "We were making our rounds when we noticed the lights were on inside

Major General Lukin's dacha and the curtains were blowing in the wind. As we pulled in, it was clear something had happened. There was glass everywhere. All the windows were broken—even the windows of the SUV parked in front of the garage. We parked the UAZ and took a closer look. When we saw blood inside the vehicle, we raced inside. That's when we found the bodies."

The memory of what he'd seen started to crack his stony façade. He took a breath to steady himself but before he could continue, Yastrzhembsky held up his hand. "You don't need to describe it. I'll see for myself. Did you see anyone or anything in or around the house?"

Michurin shook his head. "No, sir,"

"Did either of you touch anything or remove anything from the premises?"

"No, sir. We got out of there and immediately called it in once we saw…it," he gladly elided over the gory details. "Your men arrived an hour later. We've been waiting in here ever since."

"What time did all this happen?"

"A little after 1:30. We do patrol on the half hour every other hour throughout the night, and it was during the first pass. It usually takes ten minutes to drive the circuit, and Major General Lukin's dacha is on the far side of the lake. Your men relieved us around 2:30."

"You both go on patrol? Who guards the station when you

are away?"

"No one. We place the bollards up and the screen in our UAZ feeds the entrance camera to us as we patrol. If anyone arrives during that time, we use the speaker next to the camera to inform them of the delay."

"But that doesn't happen often. Those who use the dachas know our patrol times and don't arrive when we're not at the station," Gmelin added, not realizing that was in and of itself a security lapse. Michurin, however, did and gave him a sharp look to shut up and let him do the talking.

"Do you recall anything out of the ordinary leading up to the discovery?"

"No suspicious persons or vehicles, no loud noises or explosions that would account for the structural damage at the dacha," Michurin replied.

"Do you recall what time the major general arrived at the dacha and if he was alone?"

Michurin shook his head. "It wasn't during our shift. It must have been sometime before 10:00 pm." Gmelin agreed without speaking.

Yastrzhembsky curtly nodded. These men could have easily been charmed, but cameras? Not so much. It would be simple enough to review the video feed as long as it had not been tampered with. With the interview completed, he coiled up his will and unleashed it, marking each man's third eye with an arcane seal. "Under the circumstances, we must keep the details of the major general's passing secret. You will not speak, write, or otherwise express or communicate what you have seen tonight. Is that understood?"

"Yes, sir," they said emphatically. A geas of silence was no trivial thing and Yastrzhembsky didn't take such an action lightly. It was a mark they would carry for the rest of their lives—a shared secret they could not talk about, even amongst themselves.

"Good. Consider yourself relieved for the rest of your shift. Go home and get some rest," he said loud enough for the others to hear as he exited the station. With their silence magically compelled, it was time to cut them loose and see what happened. Their backgrounds would be triple-checked and their movements and contacts monitored. If they were somehow involved, it would be uncovered; he didn't believe them smart enough to have hidden all of their tracks.

Back in his SUV, he ordered his driver to make a complete circuit around the lake before stopping at Lukin's dacha. The guard station covered the only official point of entry into the community, but he knew from experience there were other ways. The lake was a popular year-round attraction—from boating in summer to ice fishing in winter—and the waterfront distinguished these vacation homes from the plebian affairs centered on gardens.

An outlet connected the lake to a small river that fed into the Moscow Canal half a kilometer away—a large canal that linked the Moskva and Volga Rivers. It made shipping from the Sea of Azov all the way to St. Petersburg possible as part of the United Deep Waterway System, but Yastrzhembsky wasn't thinking about its mercantile value. Its proximity to the lake made it a good way to enter the dacha community unobserved. It was how the squad who'd taken care of Volsky had got in.

He had his driver stop when he saw a swath of foliage along the outlet had been flattened. Greatly reduced water flow over recent dry years had rendered the area a marsh and the dead stalks of cattails and other semi-aquatic plants should be poking through the ice. Someone had knocked them down and the disturbance was too coincidental for him to discount it.

He pulled out the high-powered flashlight kept in the under-seat storage and got out to take a closer look. The first thing that struck him as odd was the lack of footprints or tracks in the snow. It had been snowing on and off all day. Even though the snow hadn't been heavy, if someone had walked this way, there should still be divots. As he looked over the area, he realized there was no snow on the icy crust of the leveled marsh and the snow was piled on either side. In a way, it reminded him of the streets of the city after a plow had passed.

A snow blower operated by someone without leaving a trace? he postulated the improbable. *Anything is possible with magic*, he reminded himself, and resolved to have someone investigate it as a possible point of entry/exit. He rubbed his hands in the warmth of the heater as he proceeded to Lukin's dacha. There were several black SUVs parked along the street with plenty of armed and uniformed muscle to discourage any curious neighbors from poking around. They all saluted him, but Spassky was the first to greet him.

Nikodim Mikhaylovich Spassky was a short, fat man with a horseshoe of hair around his mostly-bald head. His face was frozen in a sour expression, like a person who perpetually smells manure in the air. Yastrzhembsky had never seen the man smile, not even at social functions. He was, however, hardworking and observant. As a general rule, the KMB were not the Ivory Tower's best—those became field agents—and subsequently, the KMB were not as robustly trained and spent more time on the investigative aspects of the Tower's role in protecting and expanding Russian interests. Spassky was an exception, and Yastrzhembsky had recognized his value early on and kept him close.

Yastrzhembsky put the soldiers at ease and skipped the pleasantries with Spassky. "Show me." Spassky took no offense as he was also keen to get down to business.

"As ordered, we've left the scene untouched," Spassky prefaced before showing him the SUV with the blown-out windows. There was indeed glass everywhere, but none inside the vehicle. The blood splatter on the upholstery was consistent with a driver's side headshot.

"No body?"

"Inside with the chairman's," Spassky explained without giving anything away. He'd taken great strides to keep the men outside in the dark while waiting for the major general.

"Take me to him," Yastrzhembsky ordered. He followed the bald pate past the armed guards at the door into the living room, where a man had been nailed to the ceiling with four iron spikes driven through his hands and feet. The muscles of his arms and legs had been systematically severed at one end but remained attached at the other. They dangled from the corpse like a macabre chandelier. A lone triskelion had been etched on each exposed bone, including the frontal and temporal bones of the skull. There was no question it was Lukin—although peeled back, the face was still attached, albeit without a nose. That had been destroyed by a bullet's passage.

Beneath Lukin's body was the driver, an ex-field agent who'd been taken out of service after a particularly brutal mission left him unable to run. Lukin had personally chosen him, as he'd been a good agent. Now he was lying on his back beneath Lukin, desecrated in the same fashion except his muscles were fanned out like a blooming flower. Yastrzhembsky cursed—not because he'd never seen something so heinous, but because it was never supposed to happen on Russian soil.

"Who else has seen this?"

"Just the guards who found them, myself, Proskuriakova, and Alexandrov," Spassky replied at the major general's bark.

"Good. I've taken care of the guards and after the

investigation is finished, the three of you will personally remove the bodies before the cleaners arrive. We must keep this contained, even after the news of Chairman Lukin's passing is publicly announced."

"We're ready to start," Spassky said eagerly.

"Oh, your team won't be doing the investigation," Yastrzhembsky clarified. "There's only one person with any chance of untangling this knot: the Siberian."

"He's real?" Spassky questioned before his good sense had a chance to stop the words from coming out of his mouth.

"Quite," Yastrzhembsky reassured him through gritted teeth. He wasn't happy about calling him in, but that didn't change the necessity.

"What would you like us to do?" Spassky tactfully inquired. He'd already been waiting for hours and he was tired of babysitting the crime scene instead of investigating it. While he understood the importance of keeping this under wraps, it seemed a waste of his talents. He was the best in Moscow…and if one was the best in Moscow, one was the best in Russia.

"There's a trail of downed foliage in the lake's drainage outlet—I suspect that was the point of entry. See if there is anything there to be magically gleaned but have someone here to ensure no one else sees this. It would also help to establish a timeline of Lukin's movements and when his driver arrived. There's a camera at the guard station that should have timestamped video," Yastrzhembsky suggested.

Spassky was buoyed by the prospect of finally doing something. "Understood. When should we expect the Siberian to arrive?"

The Siberian keeps his own time, Yastrzhembsky thought but gave his KMB pet a more concrete answer. "I don't know. Just wait. Touch nothing."

Chapter Four

A hundred miles east of Moscow, abutting the Meshchyora National Park, was a ten-hectare parcel of land that Ivan Dmitrivich Rasputin called home. It was a more forgiving land than his native Tyumen Oblast in Western Siberia—the origin of his moniker. It was easy living compared to where he came from, with ample food from hunting, gathering, fishing, and tending his small garden. It allowed him to spend more time in prayer and meditation. To whom he prayed he would not reveal, but sometimes, when in the throes of religious ecstasy, the hundreds of black sigils tattooed over every inch of his body glowed. Unlike the cassocked dupes in the lands that surrounded him, his prayers were heard and answered. What he worshipped actually cared about him.

He lived alone in a log cabin chinked with moss that was now growing its own moss. He'd built and carved its ornamentation himself. His larder was a few meters away from the cabin: a bear cache perched on two posts he'd carved to resemble chicken legs. A small pier jutted out into the nearby lake, to which was tied a small shallow-draft boat that he had also made. From the lake, he could access many of the marshes in the area where there was an abundance of fowl in season.

Tall trees surrounded his homestead, blocking out much of the sky, and he heard the *thump-thump-thump* of the Mi-24 long before he could see it. He didn't immediately react—helicopter flyovers were not that uncommon—but he figured something was up when it circled his property before descending into a clearing by the lake. He frowned. He didn't like visitors, particularly the military kind. He'd given all he was willing to give to Mother Russia in the winter of '42; the last of his patriotism had died in Stalingrad, buried under a pile of rubble that had once been a school. Unwelcome memories of that deep winter stoked his ire.

As the chopper touched ground and powered down, he clamped down on his emotion and girded for company. Whoever it was, they knew where to find him. When the general secretary of the Ivory Tower's Interior Council appeared on the path leading to his homestead, his interested was piqued. This was no disposable colonel or major who'd bitten off more than they could chew. As far as Russian military went, Yastrzhembsky was less likely to waste his time with foolishness because he was not ignorant of who the Siberian was and what his services would cost.

As Yastrzhembsky approached, he could feel the heaviness that hung over the Siberian's home. It intensified when he could actually see the man himself, even though the Siberian wasn't much to look at. He was of average height with bushy eyebrows and a long black beard that had a few strands of gray in it. His frame was wiry: equal parts hard-working peasant and contemplative ascetic. He was sitting on a rough chair on the porch of the cabin, dressed in homemade moose-leather pants and boots. His shirt was a homemade flax *rubakha* that was only lightly decorated with embroidery. His clothing hid most of the tattoos that covered his body, but there was no escaping his eyes. They hinted that the Siberian had, in some way, transcended the shared humanity found across the cities and fields of the rest of the world. They pierced one's soul while remaining entirely indifferent to such things. Their pure, clear cerulean was as comforting as nihilism. Yastrzhembsky was not entirely convinced the Siberian hailed from *that* Rasputin heritage, but he had an undeniable puissance. His domain was a dark place, and he was one with that darkness.

The Siberian remained seated. "What brings you to my home, Nikolay?"

Being addressed informally grated on Yastrzhembsky. There was no warmth nor affection there. It was an elder calling out a subordinate. He forewent false pleasantries and cut to the chase. "Your Goshawk has broken our arrangement."

The accusation startled the Siberian. Ian Lancaster, AKA the Goshawk, was one of the few practitioner hitmen who specialized in killing magicians. The Siberian had adopted him and trained him from a young age, and the Ivory Tower agreed to leave him alone as long as he operated outside Russia and didn't accept jobs against Tower agents. There was a long silence as he stared at Yastrzhembsky, peeling back unseen layers to see if he was lying. He finally spoke when he was sure that Yastrzhembsky believed what he was saying. "What you say is not possible. My Yanchik is dead."

That was news to Yastrzhembsky, and it was his turn to see if the Siberian was bluffing…but the pained way he'd said Yanchik rang true. It was the diminutive form of Yan, the Russian version of Ian. To the Siberian, Lancaster would always be Yanchik. "You know this for a fact?"

"Yes. If he were alive, my son would not leave me in such a long silence. It has been many years since he's spoken to me."

Yastrzhembsky stared at the symbol tattooed upon the Siberian's forehead: a match to the one found on the bodies at the dacha. "And yet the triskelion is carved on the bones of the chairman of the Ivory Tower," he laid out the facts.

"The chairman?" The Siberian shook his head. "Then it is definitely not Yanchik. He would never have been so foolish."

Yastrzhembsky shrugged ."Be that as it may, what has happened has happened, and that is why I am here. I'd like you to come with me and investigate the matter. There is no one more familiar with his work than you. If someone is copying his methods, who better to spot the counterfeit than his master?" he angled for cooperation.

The Siberian saw what he was doing, but the hook found purchase, nevertheless. "I do not enter cities." The answer wasn't no, but he had stipulations.

Yastrzhembsky quickly recognized a negotiation was taking place. "Chairman Lukin was killed at his lakeside dacha. It's very exclusive—only a dozen houses around the whole lake—and we'll take a chopper there and back."

The Siberian stared off into the woods. "Is your pilot a man or one of the cattle?"

It took Yastrzhembsky a second to figure out what was being asked. "The pilot is a practitioner."

The Siberian leaned in, leading with his unwavering gaze. "Is he a real one? Does he have the stomach to do what must be done?"

"Yes," Yastrzhembsky replied, hoping he sounded more certain than he was. He didn't know what he was signing up for, but he knew that was the correct answer if he wanted the Siberian to investigate the bodies. If there was a new player in the world of magical assassination, he wanted to know sooner rather than later. He had well-funded enemies.

The Siberian sat back. "Then my price is another hectare of land to be added to what I own—on the east side, where the hunting is best."

"That's not going to be easy. It's part of the park."

The Siberian stood firm on his price. "I did not ask if it was easy. All things are possible when it is men who decide what is and isn't part of the park."

"Done," Yastrzhembsky promised and held out his hand. He'd figure out how to make it happen, but that was a problem for later. He almost flinched at the touch of the Siberian's hand. It was leathery and it prickled, as if he was holding the tongue of a great cat.

"Bentback, reveal yourself!" The Siberian commanded.

"I am here, master," a meek voice answered from a twisted imp that appeared beneath the seat of his chair. It was a small creature no taller than a housecat, nearly bent in half from extreme kyphosis. It only had two fingers and a thumb on each hand: the rest were mere stumps. The hair on his head was like that of a boar's and his thin greasy beard did little to hide the mutilated horror that had once been his genitals. The bits that remained made Yastrzhembsky look away all that much faster.

A cruel smile flashed across the Siberian's face, briefly showing his filed and blackened teeth. "Does Bentback disturb you, General Secretary?" he asked, finally rising from his chair.

"No," Yastrzhembsky made a show of strength and told himself he'd seen worse...he just hadn't had time to prepare himself.

The Siberian kicked the imp hard, sending him flying against the wall. Bentback howled in pain from both impacts. "He disturbs me constantly. He is very noisy, as you can hear." He faced the screaming imp. "Be quiet, Bentback, if you wish to keep some of your fingers." The imp's cries abruptly stopped.

"Good. Fetch the rope and bring it to the cellar door."

The imp dashed into the dim cabin. Despite its modest size, the sunlight didn't penetrate far beyond its threshold. Yastrzhembsky followed the Siberian as he started toward the back of the structure. The sense of dread that pervaded the homestead reached a pitch outside the doors leading down to the cellar. *Something* was down there, something so bad that even the Siberian left the door closed. Bentback returned with a rope trailing behind him: roughly twelve feet long with thick silver bands that prevented the ends from unraveling. It reeked of necromancy.

The Siberian sensed the general secretary's curiosity. "A rope of the damned, ritually made of braided human hair taken from the exhumed corpses of murderers." He held it up so that Yastrzhembsky could get a good look at it. He'd heard of it but had never seen one before; he wondered how many graves had been raided to make such a thing. While he did not share the Siberian's macabre interest, he couldn't fault the craftsmanship.

The Siberian coiled it around his arm and elbow and pulled on the carved wooden handle of the cellar door, releasing an awful stench. On the interior of the cellar door were dozens of wards, of which Yastrzhembsky recognized only half. The Siberian descended the steep, narrow stairs with practiced ease, but Yastrzhembsky had to take care. There was more to the darkness here; if the cabin was dim, the cellar was an abyss.

There was a jumble of woodworking tools near the stairs,

and most of the back housed a rack. Stretched along its length was a lush female body barely over five feet tall with a sigiled silver shackle binding each limb. A shiver of fear ran down Yastrzhembsky's spine when she lifted her bald head. She had no nose or ears, and the skin on her skull was as taut to the bones as if lacquered upon them. The eyes were vertically-irised, and a soft purple glow radiated within them.

A ghul was a powerful creature of undeath; even fully constrained, Yastrzhembsky could feel her endless hunger in her stare. She chomped at the air between them, demonstrating that if released, she would instantly attempt to consume him. Much to his horror, he felt his loins stir with each snap. He had to exert his will to tamp down the rising desire.

"Major General Nikolay Yastrzhembsky," the Siberian deliberately gave the general secretary's full name to the creature upon the rack, "meet my Biyaban. I acquired her during the failed war in Afghanistan. She will tell us that the assassin who killed your Lukin was not my Yanchik." He skillfully made a hangman's noose out of the rope of the damned and wrapped it around the ghul's head and cautioned Yastrzhembsky, "Do nothing that causes me to release hold of this rope. If that happens, Biyaban will be freed until one of us can catch the other end. It will not be pleasant."

He waited until Yastrzhembsky gave him a sign of comprehension before releasing each of the silver shackles. The ghul continued to snap at the air, but she docilely followed the Siberian's verbal command to get off the table and follow them out of the cellar. At the top, he closed the door with his foot and called to his imp, "Bentback, climb aboard, we are leaving!" The broken little devil climbed upon the shoulder of the ghul, impervious to her charms.

Yastrzhembsky stepped ahead of them. "Could you wait a few minutes while I go ahead? I didn't expect so many passengers and I'll need to make preparations for your entourage."

The Siberian was put out but acquiesced. "Make it quick."

The major general was working out how to explain the situation to the pilot as he hustled down the path. Then, he considered all that had to be done on the scene before the helicopter arrived at the dacha—it was one thing to bring the Siberian, but an imp and a ghul?

It pleased the Siberian to see his visitor perturbed, and a smug smile crept over his face. He gently stroked Biyaban's shoulder. "Be good and you will be rewarded when we return."

Chapter Five

Moscow Outskirts, Russia
5th of March, 11:49 a.m. (GMT+3)

There was no chatter inside the cabin of the helicopter. The Siberian stared out the window as the land rolled by beneath them, as did Bentback from the shoulder of the ghul. Biyaban, however, was less impressed with the miracle of flight. She never stopped starting at the major general, periodically opening and closing her maw in his direction. He found her gaze no less disturbing in the sunlight. Each time she tested the Siberian's hold on her leash, she was disappointed at how firm his grasp was.

The Mil Mi-24 helicopter barely fit onto the yard between the dacha and the lake, but the pilot made the landing without fuss. He was a professional who'd managed to keep it together the whole flight and it helped that there were no wires to avoid. He killed the rotors as soon as they touched the ground, hoping that it would entice his passengers to disembark that much faster.

Yastrzhembsky was first out of the helicopter to ensure his

instructions had been carried out. Spassky was waiting for him just outside the dacha. "Is everyone gone?"

"Yes, sir," Spassky replied. As ordered, he'd sent the others to the guard station until the all-clear was given. There had been a lot of grumbling, particularly as lunch was coming on and they'd been there since before breakfast, but no one dared disobey or complain. He could be very persuasive when he wanted to be.

"Good. I'll go get the Siberian. Prepare yourself…he keeps unusual company," Yastrzhembsky warned him.

Spassky calmed the butterflies in his stomach and bolstered his will. As senior KMB, he alone was allowed to be here, and it wasn't every day he got to meet a living legend. The rumors about the Siberian were as plentiful as rabbits in summer: every Ivory Tower recruit had heard them all. Supposedly, he was a grandson of the great Grigori Yefimovich Rasputin and like him, a master of the Left Hand Path of Helena Blavatsky. However, unlike his grandfather, who'd merged the Left Hand Path with Russian Orthodox Church mysticism, the Siberian had foresworn all ties to God and Country and spent his days worshiping the primordial devils and demons of the endless Russian forest.

It was said he lived alone in a cabin that was never quite in the same place twice and had more rooms on the inside than it should have. On holy days, he was visited by a *chort* that whispered secrets into his ear while he slept and who made him *zavarka* in the morning, which the Siberian mixed with the blood of children warmed in a samovar made from a mammoth's tusk. But the Siberian's greatest attribute to the young men suffering through the Tower's training program was that he was a free man. Mother Russia made no claims upon him, nor did the Ivory Tower. His arcane prowess was so great that he lived a life of his own choosing, coming and going as he willed. There wasn't a single recruit who did not long for the power to forge a destiny unfettered from all ties that bound.

The Siberian disembarked and stretched as his ghul and imp joined him in the fresh air. The change in scenery distracted Biyaban from her obsession with the general secretary. She crawled around, sniffing and biting at the new air. Bentback scuttled after her, periodically licking whatever crossed his path: a plant, a piece of glass, a patch of bare ground. His sunken and compressed chest wheezed at the effort.

At the trio investigated the environs, Yastrzhembsky stood to one side with his hands folded in front of him. Spassky tried to mimic his superior's stony expression, but it was hard to stay neutral. He'd expected the Siberian to be an elderly man, not the vital and vigorous figure in front of him. If the stories were true, Rasputin was well past his 80s, if not older. Then, there were his pets. Spassky had battled undead creatures before, but nothing like Biyaban. He was both drawn to and repulsed by her. The fact that she seemed as comfortable on all fours as she did walking on her legs bothered him on a primal level. Even the imp turned his stomach. He'd encountered them before—the Ivory Tower used them in normal operations—but never one in such a pathetic, abused state.

The ghul spoke first but in a bizarre language unknown to Yastrzhembsky and Spassky. The Siberian, however, understood and there was brief exchange between them before he translated for the others. "The attacker was human."

"Definitely human," Bentback confirmed in Russian. The imp looked to his master for permission to speak further before adding, "And a grand elemental has been here as well."

Spassky cleared his throat. "That is consistent with what we found at the lake's outlet, sir. We're assuming it was an air elemental based on the flattened vegetation and the wind-swept appearance of the snow."

Yastrzhembsky nodded. "And our killer used it to disperse any forensic evidence they may have left behind." An air elemental could create a localized explosion without the use of explosives, and it would account for all the broken windows and why the glass was blown outward.

Spassky uncomfortably shifted his weight as Biyaban took interest in him. As her vertical irises zeroed in on him, he found himself enamored by the gorgeous shade of purple that captured the soft glow from her eyes. The spell was broken with a sharp tug on the rope of the damned, and the ghul returned faithfully to the Siberian's side.

"Perhaps it's time to see the bodies. She acts up when she's bored."

Spassky shook himself. "Of course, this way." He opened the door and led them to the living room, taking a stance on the far side to put as much distance between him and the ghul as he could.

The Siberian paused at the threshold and got his first look at the two bodies. It certainly looked like Yanchik's work and he understood why the general secretary had been so adamant at his cabin. He issued an order to Biyaban and she leapt up to the ceiling. She sniffed and bit as she crawled around Lukin's corpse, indifferent to gravity's pull. Bentback licked everything in sight on the floor. Rasputin focused his piercing blue eyes to see the unseen.

The desecration had been thorough. They were not just dead; they were beyond reach. There would be no way he could communicate with them. The triskelions etched into the bones were placed precisely where they should be and the distinct orientation of their whorls was aligned to the cardinal directions. He could feel the magic coming off of them—a magic he'd invented and passed on to his adopted son, a ritual that prevented other magic from binding to the corpses. There would be no way to scry or divine what had happened here, not even for him. Biyaban and Bentback confirmed his suspicions—everything had been made too esoterically slippery for them to touch it long enough to glean anything.

He kept it to himself for the moment and asked to see

more. "This is where they were laid out. Where were they actually killed?"

"The driver was shot in his SUV and the chairmen in his bedroom," Spassky fielded the question.

"They were shot? Yanchik did not need such weapons to kill," the Siberian objected, clinging to any shred of evidence that pointed the finger away from his adopted son.

"Perhaps he thought it prudent to forego his normal methodology given the experience of the target," Yastrzhembsky offered a plausible rebuttal. "Lukin was not your average magician; he was a highly trained field agent with decades of life-or-death experience."

Rasputin shook his head but said nothing. The idea wasn't that far-fetched. Lukin had been—in his own lesser way—exceptional, and Yanchik had never been a fool who refused to adapt to circumstances.

They had just entered Lukin's bedroom when Biyaban became animated. She pulled at the rope of the damned, eager to get to the far corner of the room. Rasputin followed her lead like she was a hound on a fox hunt. The more she sniffed and snapped, the more she babbled in the same incomprehensible tongue as before. Bentback licked the upholstery and the carpet and backed her up.

"What are they saying?" Yastrzhembsky demanded to know.

Rasputin let his pets continue sniffing and licking that

which held their interest while he spoke to the major general. "A dead man did this."

"What does *that* mean?"

"It means we may very well both be right," he reluctantly admitted. "If my Yanchik has returned, he's not what he once was and he's been very naughty." He looked out the open windows, breath steaming like a dragon in the cold. "There is a way to find out more. You must take me back to my cabin immediately."

"Is there nothing else to be learned here?" Yastrzhembsky asked to make sure. The Siberian shook his head resolutely. "Very well, the chopper is waiting for us."

He turned to Spassky. "As soon as we take off, get your men in here and take care of the bodies. Not a word about the chairman's death until we know more. Understood?"

"Yes, sir."

The Siberian yanked at Biyaban's leash until she obeyed her master—whatever she sensed, it was far more captivating than the prospect of consuming Yastrzhembsky, for which the general secretary was thankful. Bentback hopped on her shoulder and the menagerie left the dacha to Spassky.

When his men arrived, he was still processing what he'd experienced. They were naturally curious, but whenever they asked, all he answered with was, "It's difficult to say." He tried very hard to make sure his voice didn't crack. He wasn't sure he succeeded.

Chapter Six

Detroit, Michigan
7th March, 6:00 a.m. (GMT-5)

The moment Penelope, once-queen of Ithica, realized she was awake, she mentally repeated the mantra Circe had instilled upon her more than three thousand years ago: *No one is immortal.* She'd lost count of how many dawns she'd greeted that way—a reminder that all creatures' days are numbered, no matter how large that number may be. The fates decreed the order of the universe, and every day was a gift to cherish, even when it felt like a burden to bear.

The practice had grounded her during her development as a power under the witch's tutelage. Transitioning from a practitioner into a power was a rare and dangerous thing. Many simply didn't have the raw talent, and of those who did, the vast majority died when tested. Of the survivors, the first hundred years—give or take a decade—were relatively safe because the newly-born power still felt fully human, even as their abilities matured beyond human capabilities.

The first reaping of fledgling powers usually occurred after the second or third human lifespan, as they started to lose touch with their humanity. Mortality seemed like a petty concern that didn't apply to them as they persisted while generations of people came and went. They slowly ceased doing the protective behaviors that had gotten them so far in the first place. They got sloppy with their power because they had so much of it throw about, especially in comparison to those around them. They would slip up and die in stupid and foolish ways. But not Penelope, and she credited her mentor for her continued survival.

After the hundredth anniversary of Circe's death, she'd added an addendum to the mantra: *But I'm not dead yet.* It was her affirmation to make hay while the sun shined upon her still-living face, or as the murderous Romans would put it, *carpe diem.* She was not one of the fates: the future was unknown to her and yet to happen, which meant she could still affect it. It was her way of combating the listlessness that accumulated century after century—a rejection of the dulling comfort of predestination that had taken the ancient witch who'd trained her. In a seemingly endless present, she started each day asking herself the two questions that really mattered: What promises are you making? How are you going to keep them?

She opened her eyes and the familiar surroundings immediately oriented her in time, place, and person. She was Angelica Zervo, the CEO of Discretion Minerals, a CIA-owned cover for the Salt Mine—a secret black books organization that policed and contained magical threats. And she was their Leader. As she pushed aside the snow white sheepskins and rose from her linen bed, she swore she was not going to get herself killed today. If the fates cut her string, it would be the inescapable outcome of existing in an indifferent universe, not the result of a poor decision on her part. Driven by the notion that there was a tomorrow that was worth showing up for, she would not succumb to the malaise of the inevitable. That was the promise she made to herself at the beginning of this new day.

Angelica Zervo's apartment occupied the entire top floor of the Ithikis Building, a twenty-seven-story luxury residential tower. She'd built the structure to her exacting standards in the 1970s via various holding companies under her control. She had a private elevator to the penthouse and a helicopter pad for those times when she needed to get away quickly. Because she kept the Beaux-Arts/Neoclassical style of its predecessor—the unfortunately named Barium Tower—it blended in with the other Detroit skyscrapers, and casual passersby assumed it was a much older building.

The internals had been modernized several times since its initial construction, but the magical protections required no renovation. The wards might not be as elegant as Fulcrum's beloved 500, but they were far more robust and powerful. Fulcrum's penchant for seamless engineering left an antagonist puzzling how to bypass his wards, the metaphysical equivalent of contorting one's self across a field of laser beams in a heist movie. Anyone trying to get past the Ithikis Building's arcane protections would just wonder how they were supposed to generate enough power to put a dent in them.

Her bedroom was in the middle of the building, encased in several feet of reinforced concrete. It was as much of a bunker or safe room as one could create at elevation. The absence of windows meant it could be made completely dark at any hour, allowing her to sleep whenever she wished. She raised her will and a single flickering light appeared. Its luminescence was soft, more like a candle than an electric light bulb. She put on her robe and opened the heavy, reinforced door. It swung smoothly on quiet hinges onto a long hallway that pointed east. Based on the color of the sky, the sun would make its appearance in about an hour.

She performed her ablutions in the bathroom to the reflection she currently called her own. She'd long mastered the ritual to alter herself. While many used such magic to preserve the bloom of youth, she was less concerned with vanity. She allowed each face and body she adopted to age until it was time to take on a new persona. She'd been young, middle-aged, and old many times over, living numerous variants of the life of a woman for eons. According to her official documents, Angelica Zervo was a seasoned businesswoman of sixty-three years: invisible when she wanted to be, but too old to put up with anyone's shit. In another time, she'd have chosen a younger, more fetching body to wield soft power, but thankfully, she'd outlived the most egregious of those days. She did not miss the times when females were merely an appendage of father, brother, husband, or son.

In the kitchen, she turned on recorded birdsongs of India and made herself breakfast: two eggs fried in olive oil, a thick slice of homemade barley bread dipped in wine, and two fresh figs over which was drizzled a small amount of honey. She sat at the head of a long table with a small glass of water as her only liquid. She took small bites, taking time to thoroughly chew her food before swallowing. Outside, the dark sky continued to brighten and as if on cue, the distinctive cry of a peacock sounded. She smiled at fond memories of her time in the subcontinent; how many mornings had that call been her alarm?

After eating, she cleared the dishes and made a cup of coffee and settled in with her tablet. Once she saw she had no official communiqués flagged as urgent, she dove into the shallow end of the web for twenty minutes. All the important world events would be covered at the office, but it was equally important to remain current with American pop culture, at least that part of it that a woman in her sixties would care about. The internet made the task much easier.

As she scrolled through reviews of movies and TV shows, she sipped her coffee until it became cool enough to drink in earnest. With a tap of her finger, she matched names with faces and lamented what counted as fashionable these days. She skimmed the top ten of the largest music genres, new releases in literature and non-fiction, and what was taking the art world by storm—nothing extensive, but enough to recognize titles and creators. Last, she read the headlines in science and technology.

Occasionally, she found something that sounded interesting and took a deeper look. Today, it was the discovery of a milk-producing amphibian in Brazil. The mental image in her head did not match the pictures published with the article. The amphibian was something called a caecilian, a worm-like subterranean creature with lots of wriggling young nestled in its folds. While not technically milk, the lipid and sugar-laden substance exuded out of their tail was serving a similar purpose: how to feed offspring that are born long before they can take care of themselves. *Life finds a way…*

She decided against starting her dailies when she saw the time in the corner of the screen. After a quick rinse, she put her coffee mug in the dishwasher and got ready for work. Mondays were when she took care of Discretion Minerals, which a real company that required tending. However, it had fewer moving parts and much less in jeopardy than the Salt Mine. With the help of Ethan Helms, her above-ground assistant, she could get a week's worth of work done in a day. It was a damning comment on the average CEO's profligacy with time. Sure, most did not have her prodigious experience or her ability to grease the wheels with magic, but she also wasn't coming in late, taking two-hour lunches, and leaving early to golf.

She applied a bit of makeup and put on a navy pantsuit with a string of pearls. She slid her feet into a pair of pumps and grabbed her bag on the way out. She rode her private elevator down to her private garage—a part of the basement that had been sequestered from the other residents' vehicles. Waiting for her beside a black bulletproof SUV was her bodyguard-slash-assistant, David LaSalle. At a little over five feet tall, she seemed comically small against the brick of muscle, but he treated her with nothing but respect.

"Good morning, ma'am," he greeted her as he opened the door for her.

"Morning, David. Anything of note?" It was her way of inquiring about the kind of things that were important but wouldn't show up in her briefings. He generally knew everything going on in the Salt Mine—including its agents' private lives—and he had a knack for sussing out germane intel from hot gossip for which she didn't care.

He shook his head. "Nothing new." She settled in as he closed the door behind her and climbed into the driver's seat. As he drove them to Zug Island, she started reading the dailies. Halfway there, she got to an Ivory Tower update. There had been a significant uptick in encrypted SIGINT regarding the cancellation of an important meeting due to Chairman Lukin's sudden illness. He was supposed to chair the summit, and there were some high-ranking military on the attendee list: the minister of defense, the chief of the general staff, and the general in command of the Southern Military District. The precise agenda was unknown, but it would certainly involve the recent infiltration of Ivory Tower agents into the Ukraine army and their subsequent discovery and destruction by the Salt Mine's Hobgoblin.

Spikes in encrypted communication happened with some frequency, but the content of the message paired with the stated reason for cancellation was suspicious. If Lukin was simply sick, there was no need to be so secretive about it. Meetings got canceled and rescheduled all the time. *Perhaps this is something I should look into personally…*

The analysts were very good at gathering data, but she had private sources within the Ivory Tower whom she could ask. Because each contact came with the threat of discovery, she rarely communicated with them, but so far, they had been reliable. The crux of the matter came down to this: was the information to be gained important enough to justify the risk? As LaSalle stopped at the security gate and presented his ID to the guard, she decided to let the issue simmer on the back burner while she took care of Zervo's business obligations.

Chapter Seven

Buttercrambe Hall, Yorkshire, UK
7th March, 3:25 p.m. (GMT)

Cordelia Rosamund Camise Durand Leek, Countess of Stamford, brushed aside the curtains of her third-story bedroom window and stole a glance at the festivities below. The gardens of Buttercrambe Hall, festooned in the family colors of gold and black, gleamed in the sunlight of clear and temperate skies. Yorkshire in March was not ideal for an outdoor event, but the Leeks were never one to allow something as insignificant as the weather to get in the way of their plans. What was the point of having generational magical wealth if one did not occasionally use it to make sure that special days were not ruined by dreary low-hanging clouds and rain that never seemed more than a few hours away?

The Yorkshire Leeks were one of the oldest magical families in the UK, and *the* wealthiest. They could trace their lineage back to the Viking chief Ubba, who'd landed in East Anglia with the Great Heathen Army in 865. In 866 the army sacked York, and Ubba produced a by-blow off one of the Northumbrian natives. That son was considered the first true Leek born on English soil, and ever since, the family had played an important role in politics, peaking in the sixteenth to nineteenth centuries.

While the Leeks owned many properties throughout the UK as well as on the continent, the heart of their holdings was Buttercrambe Hall. While other great families had been forced to relinquish their grand ancestral homes, the Leeks held fast to what was theirs. Over a hundred yards in breadth and three lofty stories tall, Buttercrambe Hall stood in dominion over a three-hundred-acre property. The majestic Gothic Revival great house was built in 1786 after a fire had consumed most of the house that had previously stood there. It held one hundred seventy-five rooms, forty staff bedrooms, ten offices, twenty bathrooms, and four large staterooms. Although massive, Buttercrambe Hall groaned to accommodate all of its guests on this very special occasion. Non-bedrooms had been turned into sleeping quarters for the youngest members of visiting families and the servants' quarters were packed like sardines with their help.

Guests and event staff had been arriving all day, and Cordelia was happy to stay in her room and leave the bustle to her son, Marmaduke Williams Wilson Durand Leek. When she was gone, Daunty would have to pick up the mantel, and after him, his new son, born to him by the new wife she'd found him after Vavasour's demise. He was still just a babe, but she could sense the incipient power in his infant soul—at last, a male heir worthy of the Leek name!

She scanned the lawn and found everything as it should be. The tents bearing standard tea-time favorites were erected on one side and the bandstand set up opposite it. Two servants wearing traditional livery attached a flag bearing the Leek family coat of arms to the towering flagpole. At precisely 3:30 pm, they raised a solid black flag with three golden unicorns standing on hind legs and the band began to play "Lillibullero." The 220th gathering of the Dawn Club was officially in session. She smiled at the sight of her son reverently staring at the coat of arms: *sable, three unicorns rampant or.* Even as a child, he'd been fascinated with heraldry. It was the exclusive language of his peers. He might not be much of a magician, but he knew the value of good breeding and was proud to be a Leek. That counted for something.

Despite the cheerful faces and lively music, there was a damper on the gaiety. In January, the Dawn Club had learned of a new threat to their power: the Security Service and Secret Intelligence Service were starting a joint operation called the Secret Esoteric Service. Promoting UK interests in the magical sphere had been the purview of the Club for centuries, and all the influential families were in attendance to voice their opinion on how to proceed. Personally, she was a staunch opponent of a government takeover and viewed it as an egregious overreach of MI5 and MI6. They should know better.

Her stomach rumbled as the first of the guests came out with laden plates. The cukes from the greenhouse had been surprisingly sweet this winter, and the thought of a cucumber sandwich made her salivate. Although the meeting officially started at tea time, she delayed her entrance until 4:01—the exact time of her birth. It was a practice she'd started thirty years ago when she became the Club's Ipsissimus. She did not think being born on the same day of the start of the annual meeting was a coincidence. As the unofficial head of the Dawn Club, it was her destiny to return the Leek family into prominence after decades of hard times.

She shushed the ill-mannered grumble in her tummy; now was not the time to break with tradition. *Heaven only knows how many more meetings I'll make*, she sighed. She hadn't left the estate much since the heart attack she'd suffered after Asher's passing. The doctors said she was coming along nicely, but she didn't feel recovered. One did what one must, but Imogene's recent death made it even harder to keep a stiff upper lip. Her late husband's spinster sister had been her closest confidant. The doctors had found the cancer in her liver too late and she'd passed quickly and—luckily—nearly painlessly.

A knock at the door interrupted her morbid thoughts and she pulled herself together. "Yes?"

"Lady Leek, I have a message from Sir Marmaduke," an unfamiliar voice with an accent addressed her through the door.

What does he want now? she thought, exasperated. *And who the devil is that?* Her composure was doubly tested as she tried to place the accent. With so many visitors at the Hall for the meeting, there was no way she could keep up with all the strangers. It wasn't one of her servants—she insisted on staff that could speak proper English. She didn't approve of hiring immigrants from Eastern Europe, but she couldn't control what other families did and some couldn't afford to be choosey.

"Very well, enter!" she commanded without taking her eyes off the crowd beneath her. She couldn't decide which looked more fetching: the Victoria sponge or the generously filled scones.

Behind her, the door opened and closed. "Lady Leek?"

She huffed at the quality of the help, even if it wasn't hers. Of course, she was Lady Leek! Whose room was this? Hadn't she already confirmed she was when she'd answered the knock? She released the curtain and turned to dress down the servant, but before she could say a word, she faded into unconsciousness.

At 4:00 sharp, the band played a musical fanfare, the lead-in to what should have been Cordelia's dramatic entrance. The expectant attendees readied themselves to applaud the Leek matriarch as soon as she formally joined them. When 4:01 came and went without her arrival, a hush fell over the crowd and quickly turned into a wave of whispers.

Marmaduke double-checked the time because it wasn't like his mother to be late or miss her cue. Once he was certain she wasn't coming, he stood on the stage to gain high ground and raised his voice. "Everyone, please continue to enjoy yourselves. I'll see what has delayed our esteemed hostess." He motioned for the band to move on to another song so the merriment could continue.

He moved through the guests with calculated ease to give the impression he had everything under control. It wasn't until he was inside Buttercrambe Hall that he picked up the pace. He was slightly out of breath from hustling up two flights of stairs and took a second to collect himself before knocking on his mother's bedroom door.

"Mother? The guests are waiting." When no answer came, he knocked again and spoke louder. "Is everything okay in there?" His irritation turned to fear when all was silent on the other side—had she had another heart attack?

He pushed the door open and gasped at the sight of his mother. She was dressed in a blue flock with pale yellow flowers, slumped over in her favorite chair with her blood and brains splattered against the nearby wall. A gun lay on the carpet on her right side below her dangling hand.

He ran to her in a mix of confusion and shock, his brain unable to process everything all at once. As he got closer, he saw something on the dressing table beside her: a tri-folded piece of paper propped up against the hat she'd recently bought for the garden party. Upon it was written: "My dearest Daunty." He grabbed the note, desperately searching for answers because none of it made sense. His shaky hands unfolded the thick, bespoke stationery. Inside was a single word written in black ink: *Boom*. As soon as he read it, an arcane explosion rippled out and everything went black for Marmaduke Williams Wilson Durand Leek.

Chapter Eight

Detroit, Michigan
7th March, 1:00 p.m. (GMT-5

After a busy morning of meetings, Leader was having a bit of a late lunch in Angelica Zervo's penthouse office. The expensive furnishings and aesthetic were in keeping with a CEO of a multinational mining corporation, but she preferred of the view of the river while she savored her bagel and smear loaded with lox and capers rather than that of the interior decoration.

She was on her last bite when the voice of Ethan Helms came over the intercom. "Sorry to interrupt, Ms. Zervo, but David LaSalle is here to see you."

The unscheduled appearance of her subterranean assistant prompted her to chew faster—whatever it was, it had to be important. She swallowed her food before responding. "Send him in." She crumpled up the wax paper containing all the toppings of the everything bagel that had eluded consumption and threw the wad in the waste basket.

The broad-shouldered and well-suited form of her bodyguard-slash-assistant entered but said nothing until the door was securely closed behind him. "Someone just MEMPed the Dawn Club's annual meeting."

MEMP was the name given to the arcane version of an EMP: instead of disabling electronics, it disabled magic. A magician poured their arcane energy into an object associated with a target location and allowed it to accumulate energy over time. The subsequent pent-up metaphysical force would be released all at once when the trigger was pulled—usually a designated or keyed change in state. In a fraction of a second, the resultant arcane wave stripped items of their enchantments, overwhelmed and fried wards, banished summoned creatures to their native realm, severed magically bound oaths, and left practitioners without the ability to wield magic.

The fallout from a MEMP varied: anything from a few months to permanent obliteration of magical ability, depending on the capability of the practitioner that built it and the amount of energy it had accumulated. The strongest MEMPs could even prevent magical development in as-yet-unborn generations. They were the nuclear option among magicians, and because of that, MEMPs were unanimously deemed a forbidden magic by all magical agencies and organizations across the globe. As with necromancy and time magic, they had agreed to shun their use and assist each other should one be employed. Like nuclear war, the only way to win was not to play.

"Who informed us?"

"Marmaduke Leek. He thinks it's the Secret Esoteric

Service launching a preemptive strike against the Dawn Club," he repeated what he'd been told.

Leader's left brow raised ever so slightly at the accusation. There was no need for the SES to take such drastic action against the Dawn Club. Like so many of the British ventures that had its roots in their imperial days, it would finally wither on the vine as progress passed it by, complaining loudly about how things were better when they were in charge. In her mind, it was much more likely that someone within the club set it off as a false flag. "How bad was the damage?"

"The MEMP went off half an hour after the first garden tea started. Everyone in attendance was affected. Someone just wiped out the leadership of the Dawn Club in one fell swoop," LaSalle spelled out the implications.

Leader was unable to contain her surprise and uttered a monosyllabic, "Woah."

"And there is the matter of Cordelia Leek's apparent suicide—a bullet to the head," LaSalle dropped the other shoe. "Marmaduke believes it was an assassination staged to look like a suicide because the note left with her body was the MEMP trigger."

She leaned back in her leather swivel office chair. Her mind immediately wondered who knew about the meeting and wasn't there. Who stood to gain at dethroning the current Ipsissimus and magically neutering her heir? Then, her mind made a connection to another tidbit of information that had been irritating it all morning, like a pebble lodged in one's shoe: in less than twenty-four hours, Lukin had canceled an important security meeting and Cordelia Leek was assassinated.

Leader reached over to the intercom. "Ethan, cancel all my afternoon appointments. I'll be spending the rest of the day at my other office. You have fifteen minutes to gather anything you need me to sign before I leave."

"Yes, Ms. Zervo," Helms replied calmly. He'd been expecting as much as soon as he saw her other assistant, but he knew better than to ask for details.

Then, she addressed LaSalle. "Tell Marmaduke we'll assist in the investigation—we can't have the SES look into the matter if they really are involved. Have him supply a list of who was there as well as a general member list—this is non-negotiable," she stressed. In the past, Cordelia Leek had been reluctant to relinquish any club information to the Salt Mine. "Someone on a lower rung might have seized the moment to ascend while setting up the SES to take the blame. Also, see which students stayed at Harrowgate instead of attending."

Harrowgate was the private boarding school the Dawn Club ran for their member families. It prepared its students for mundane university while also teaching them how to use their magical abilities and educating them about who their real peers were. Dawn Club meetings were deemed school holidays, but there was always the chance that some students had remained behind. If so, they'd need to be interviewed and ruled out as perpetrators. There was a reason so many of the classic stories involved children killing their parents to assume power.

"Would you like me to wait and escort you to the fourth floor?" he offered as she gathered her things.

"No. I'll be working in my other, other office," she alluded to her workshop located even lower than the fourth floor. It was where she stored the arcane tools from all her past lives, should she ever need them. He'd worked with her long enough to recognize when the conversation was over and unceremoniously left to execute her orders.

After her personal items were packed away, she tidied her desk and stacked the folders of unfinished business to one side for Helms, who already handled most of the daily operations. On her way out, she took care of the remaining documents that required her signature and left Discretion Minerals in his capable stewardship as she took the elevator down. When the Salt Mine was being constructed, she'd been tempted to give herself direct access from the penthouse to the subterranean sixth floor, but it was too much of a security gap to justify for mere convenience. Leader, like everyone else, had to go through the first floor.

Angela Abrams put away her magazine and sat up straight when she saw who was in the approaching carriage. She greeted her professionally and performed a textbook security check. The whirling seemed to take forever under those steely gray eyes and Abrams fought the urge to make nervous chitchat as the machine processed Leader's belongings. As soon as the system gave the all-clear, she opened the door and breathed a sigh of relief when she was no longer under her boss's direct observation.

Once inside, Leader presented her palm and retina to a pair of elevators and descended to the sixth floor. She walked through the various wards into the domain of Chloe and Dot to yet another elevator. This one went even deeper into the earth, where her workshop resided as well as powerful relics, artifacts, and Furfur, Great Earl of Hell. It was the most secure location in the Salt Mine because the twins were more than just the Mine's librarians and general font of arcane knowledge. They were Janus in mortal form, and she could think of no one better to guard the way than the Keeper of Gates.

She headed to the spartan bedroom in the back of her workshop where she slept when an evolving situation required her to stay close at hand. She found extra clothing in the WWII-era foot locker next to a repurposed Vietnam war-era cot and changed out of her suit and pumps into something more suitable for the ritual she was about to perform.

Near the bottom of the trunk, safely wedged between two hand-knitted sweaters, was a small oval mirror. The frame was nothing special: blackened oak sealed with several thick layers of lacquer. The mirror, however, was enchanted. Beside it were two iron shoes. They were oversized for her, but that didn't matter. They longed to be worn and would size themselves.

She hung the mirror on the wall and placed the shoes on the grill. With a simple command, a small fire elemental heated them until they were red hot. She gathered her will and wrapped it around her feet and lower legs before carefully donning the shoes. The only thing between her flesh and a thousand degrees of hot iron was her relentless discipline. She took a few steps to the mirror. "Mirror, mirror on the wall, show me that which appalls!"

As soon as she spoke the enchanted words, the curse of the iron shoes kicked in, forcing her to dance. Her feet immediately recognized the choreography. It was a dance of her youth, one that had been forgotten by time and which she alone now knew. As she moved to the *diapodia*, the mirror darkened before coming into focus on an impeccably dressed imp. His hair was immaculately coiffed and his three-piece suit bespoke for his diminutive proportions, but what really interested her was the ivory collar around his neck.

She spun the image around, surveying the area to ensure he was alone before calling him by his true name. "Fulbrecan, I name you and draw your attention!"

Even though the little imp recognized the disembodied voice, he nearly jumped out of his skin. "Quiet, someone could hear you!" he desperately whispered. "What do you want?"

"I want to know what's happening with Chairman Lukin," she said as she dipped and twirled.

"Heh, you and everyone else," the foppish imp snidely

remarked. He grinned at the prospect of knowing something she did not. The human female who had him by the short hairs might know his true name and how he'd escaped the wrath of Lord Furfur—whom he'd faithfully served until the great earl marked him for destruction—but she did not know what was common knowledge among the Ivory Tower's imp network.

She transferred some of the heat coming off her shoes and edged her words with it as she spoke his name again. "Fulbrecan, speak plainly."

The imp rankled at the command and expanded upon his previous statement. "I believe you mean *Ex-Chairman* Lukin." Complying with her request eased his discomfort as did the scope of the news. Normally, the kind of information she wanted didn't seem like a big deal to him, and he savored holding the death of a chairman over her, even if it was only for a second. It made him feel a little better about his stenotic situation.

"Lukin is dead?" she nailed him down. She'd long ago learned how litigious and exacting devils could be.

"Deader than dead. The suspicion is that he was killed by the Goshawk. Found him at his dacha late Friday all de-muscled and his bones magically ornamented and everything. His holiness Yastrzhembsky even called in the Siberian to take a look around." Fulbrecan didn't need to be forced further to spill the beans. This gossip was too juicy not to share.

Leader tucked away each piece of information for later

consideration when she was no longer forced to dance and keep back the scorching heat. Fulbrecan was beholden to her goodwill—there were much worse things she could do to him using his true name—and his words had never proven false because of it. "What did the Siberian find?"

The imp shrugged. "Don't know. No new information requests have come through since he came sniffing around with his creepy ghul."

"What about his imp?"

Sensing where she was going, he played dumb, "Greedigut?"

"No, not Lukin's. The Siberian's imp, Bentback," she specified.

"How should I know? He's not part of the network," he deflected her query.

"But he's related to someone, and every imp knows an imp who knows an imp," she pressed as sweat started beading on her brow. While the Ivory Tower regarded the imp network as little more than a biological computer that carried out its searches and stored its data, they had a societal structure of their own. Information and rumors were their currency, both within the Ivory Tower imp network and outside of it. She included his name again to formalize the order, "Fulbrecan, get the dirt from Bentback and send the information via our normal way. I want to know what the Siberian knows about Lukin's death."

"As you wish," the imp gulped. Being a mole in the Ivory

Tower was not conducive to a long life, but he was bound by his true name. All he could do was try to keep the spinning plates he had in the air from crashing down.

"Don't look so glum. If anyone can do it, it's you," she added charitably before breaking the communication. The mirror went black before reflecting her form again. She exerted her will and took control of the dance, metaphysically unraveling herself from the curse of the iron shoes. It required a finesse few could accomplish, even if they had the requisite power. After she gracefully completed the diapodia on her own accord, she slipped her feet out of the hot iron and used fireplace tongs to move them to the far corner to cool completely. With the burn threat removed, she spread herself out on the cold saline floor and caught her breath.

Goshawk was a name she hadn't heard in years, not since the Mine put him permanently out of business. Magical murder for hire was best nipped in the bud ASAP. She would love to get an agent into the dacha to saltcast—an arcane diagnostic tool that only the Salt Mine had—but it was much too risky. It wasn't just operating in the heart of Ivory Tower territory; Yastrzhembsky would have it locked down if he was trying to keep a tight lid on the news of Lukin's passing. She would have to settle on tapping into the imp network; knowing what the opponent knew—and didn't know—had its own strategic value. Once she'd cooled down, she went to another part of her workshop and rang LaSalle at his fourth-floor desk.

"David LaSalle," he answered in a crisp tenor.

"David, I want you to issue a high alert to all agents in the field," she said without introducing herself. "Also, push up installation of the security improvements Weber and Lundqvist have been working on…tonight, if possible."

"I'll see what I can do," he replied as he made notes in his own brand of shorthand.

"Any news from England?"

"The police have officially deemed Cordelia Leek's death as a suicide. Marmaduke has agreed to supply the information you requested and would like to know who we are sending to perform the *real* investigation."

Leader smiled. "Send Fulcrum."

He confirmed the message was received with a simple, "Yes, ma'am."

She placed the phone back in the cradle and decided to steal a moment for herself while she waited for the shoes to fully cool. Her faithful assistants above and below-ground were carrying out her orders and if she were lucky, Fulbrecan would send word sooner rather than later. She fished out the wand and whorl of Circe from her tortoiseshell sewing box and set to work on the cleaned and carded Vlachian wool that had yet to be spun.

As she worked, she wondered what would pair well with the bottle of wine she'd set aside for Lukin's passing. She certainly hadn't expected it to come so quickly.

Chapter Nine

David Emrys Wilson—codename Fulcrum—stepped onto his trenching tool for the umpteenth time, using his body weight to drive the blade into the lush soil. As the metal cut the sparkling burgundy mushroom from the network of mycelium, it lost its shiny chromed appearance and the color quickly drained out of it. He cast it to one side and went again, targeting the next one in the fairy ring.

Breaking the circle in the mortal realm was enough to temporarily sever the connection to the middle lands, but the portal would quickly reconnect if the enchanted mushrooms in the Magh Meall weren't also dislodged. Because it required safely entering and leaving the buffer zone between humans and fae, decommissioning fairy rings fell squarely into the purview of the Salt Mine. It wasn't a complicated task, arcanely speaking, which made it a prized assignment amongst agents.

Up until recently, Wilson would have considered this a nice break: go to North Carolina, get some good grub, and cross over to do a little light gardening in the dappled purple-tinged sunlight that slipped through the canopy while soft breezes perfumed the air with fragrant, sweet grass. However, the last time he'd depowered a fairy ring, he'd encountered a hamadryad who was quite fond of the pretty little fungi. That memory soured the otherwise idyllic environs and served as a practical reminder that deadly things could come in very attractive packages.

With some quick thinking and a considerable exertion of will, he'd managed to keep her wrath at bay and obtain vital information for the larger mission at hand. In fact, she'd been so amused with him that she'd offered him her fruits, forcing him to walk the tightrope of tactfully turning her down without offending her. He would happily go the rest of his life without being in such a position again. Leery of lingering longer than he must, he gathered his things as soon as he dug up the last mushroom and returned to the spot he'd anchored to Hatteras Island, North Carolina.

He touched his belly button with his will, looking for his antahkarana: the metaphysical thread that tethered him to the mortal realm. When he first started visiting the Magh Meall, he had to use it like a rope, pulling himself out of the enchanted land. Leaving became less taxing as he got more facile with wielding his power. Now, it was like putting one's hand on a bannister while walking down stairs—supportive but largely unnecessary unless he lost his footing.

The light changed color and the verdant green lost its intense and pure aroma as he reentered his world. He checked the time on the 1950's Bucherer travel alarm clock he used whenever he ventured into the Magh Meall: 1:27 pm. Less than thirty minutes had passed here even though he'd done at least an hour's worth of physical labor digging up the vegetation that constituted the fairy circle.

Assuming I entered at 13 o'clock, he mentally added a caveat as he drank deep from his water bottle. Ever since he'd returned from Avalon, he'd found it easier to enter the Magh Meall, sometimes shaving minutes off what had always been a strict hour of meditation. It wasn't consistent or even a given, but it was one of the many changes he'd noted. He filled in the trench and removed all traces that he'd been there. Buxton Woods was a dedicated nature preserve and he tried to follow the old adage: take only photographs and leave only footprints.

He trekked back to the home of Brianna Dare, a thirty-one-year-old woman with two small children. When her kids started prattling on about visitors, she'd assumed they meant tourists. The Outer Banks drew in lots of nature-lovers. Her suspicions arose when they started taking food from the kitchen before heading out to the woods to play because they weren't asking for normal things like snacks, more like ingredients: raw flour, salt, bulbs of garlic, dried herbs and spices. As soon as she saw the pictures they were drawing, she kept them indoors and called the hotline.

The back door flew open before he'd had a chance to knock. "Did you take care of it?" Dare asked in a hushed tone. She'd just gotten both of her kids down for a nap and heaven help the poor soul that woke them prematurely.

"Yes. Someone will come by every few years to make sure the way stays shut, but they'll go straight there—no need to bother you," Wilson reassured her. Under her supervision, the kids had shown him where the fairy ring was after he was certain they were not fae themselves.

While relieved, she kept looking for other angles before she let her guard down. "And you're sure the kids are okay?"

"I didn't find any sign they had been tampered with or marked. Should they inherit your talent, they may be drawn to faeries because of this early exposure—it's something you should warn them of as they get older. Some of the most dangerous creatures are utterly beautiful," he cautioned. "Otherwise, live your lives and call the tip line if anything strange does happen."

He did not expect the big hug she laid on him. He didn't try to dodge it, because she seemed to need it after all the worry and effort of keeping two kids with cabin-fever entertained at home. "Thank you."

"You're welcome," he said as he lightly patted her back. "I better get on the road if I'm going to catch my flight."

She took the hint and released her hold. "Drive safe, and if you're ever in these parts again, you're always welcome here."

He was on his way to the airport when his phone buzzed

with an urgent message: HIGH ALERT—GENERAL ASSASSINATION RISK ALL AGENTS. He immediately pulled over and checked his rental car. He didn't think he'd find explosives or a cut break line—if they were going to take him out that way, it would have already happened— but a tracker bug? He'd nearly finished his inspection when his mobile went off again, this time a message from LaSalle. Instead of returning to Detroit, Wilson was flying out to Dulles International and then to Liverpool, where he'd rent a car for the long drive to Buttercrambe Hall, a place he'd last visited over two years ago investigating the death of Asher Leek. He skimmed the brief for the broad strokes: Cordelia Leek assassinated and the Dawn Club meeting at Buttercrambe Hall MEMPed.

The news seemed too unreal to be true and it slowly sank in on the rest of his drive to Norfolk International. The reason for the high alert was clear. If someone had the ability and balls to hit the Dawn Club and kill its leader, all groups that monitor magic needed to be vigilant.

He wasn't able to dig into the details until after he returned his rental car and checked into his new flight. Over a so-so airport calzone, he got caught up with the Leek family. With the death of Cordelia Leek, the current master of the estate was Marmaduke Leek, age forty-eight. His first wife, Vavasour de Klerk Durand Leek, had died in a car accident not long after Wilson had concluded his investigation of their son's death. Marmaduke had since remarried to Mary Grace Yarburgh-

Bateson Leek, age twenty-four, and had a newly born son, Harry. *Wonder if he's an heir or a spare,* Wilson drily thought. If historical British dramas were to be believed, Ferris should be the next in line, but he was no practitioner. *Of course, after the MEMP, none of them might be.*

While MEMPs were technically forbidden magic, in his mind, they paled in comparison to messing with time or necromancy. Those kinds of things eroded or even destroyed the fabric of reality; an MEMP only destroyed magic. He couldn't help but admire the efficiency behind it. If he'd been given the mission of ending the Dawn Club and normal restraints had been lifted, it's what he would have done. But MEMPs were forbidden and retaliation could quickly get out of hand. He needed to play this one close to his chest.

Chapter Ten

Vladimir Oblast, Russia
7th of March, 11:59 p.m. (GMT+3)

It was close to midnight by the time the Siberian had everything ready. It was a bitterly cold night, and the campfire popped and spit from the three freshly-cut larch logs he'd just thrown upon it. He disrobed and stood naked before the roaring flames. Upon the pyre, he tossed a trussed baby goat. Its screams were not unlike that of a human child. As it died, he let its pain and fear wash over him and bathed in the pungent smoke of the wet wood. It edified him, and he focused his will into a circle encompassing himself, the fire, and the burning goat. In an instant, he was elsewhere: the realm of the mightiest servant of his master. If anyone could help him find his Yanchik, it would be She Who Teaches in Darkness.

Night had its own unique bouquet and the smell of it in the Magh Meall was intoxicating. It evoked a memory embedded deep in his soul: sneaking out as a child while his parents slept. In the darkness, he'd wander the woods alone and familiar places took on different dimensions. It was a world that could never fully belong to humans—the night and the forest—yet he felt at home in both.

He dressed and mentally prepared to cast a spell he'd learned many decades ago—one he'd only dared to cast a few times since. It wasn't something done lightly, even for one of his prowess and ethos. The first time was to swear himself to the service of the master. The last time, he'd brought his adopted son to pledge allegiance to the same dark power.

When he was ready, he inhaled deeply and started whistling. The song was quite lyrical and far more complex than the bird-summoning spell it had been based on. He modulated the pitch with his lips and will and finished with a particularly difficult trill. When he was done, a pregnant silence filled the space between the trees.

His ears picked up a noise in the distance: the distinct sound of ponderous feet moving toward him. As the repetitive thuds became louder, he gathered his courage. He could show no weakness if he wished to live. Out of the woods lumbered the dark shape of an *izba* upon its massive chicken legs. It walked around Rasputin and the fire before folding its legs beneath it and settled to the ground. Its rough-cut pine door flew open, inviting him to enter, if he dared.

He hesitated. He'd never been inside before. Its mistress had always come out during their previous encounters and the door had closed immediately after she exited, and only briefly opened for her return. Regardless of the invitation, he wasn't about to enter Baba Yaga's house without introducing himself.

He loudly proclaimed, "I am Ivan Dmitrivich Rasputin, servant of our master! We have spoken before and we will speak again!" There was no response, but because the door remained open, he bravely strode across the threshold.

The interior was cramped but cozy. A massive Russian masonry stove with an interior chamber perfectly sized for roasting children took up nearly half of the cabin. On top of the stove was a feather mattress covered with multiple patchwork quilts. Next to the warm bricks and the slightly ajar oven door was an oversized chair made of bones and joined by sinew. In the chair stood a naked toddler using the back of the chair to hold themselves up to suckle from a distended breast dangling from the low ceiling. It resembled a cow's udder more than the curvaceous mound of a woman's breast, and Rasputin realized it belonged to none other than Baba Yaga when he visually traced it back to its source: a mass of flesh stretched out across all four corners of the hut.

"Welcome," a familiar voice greeted him from behind and above.

The Siberian spun around to face an anacondian neck holding her double-sized head. Her teeth were black as wrought iron and her eyes glowed like coals in a blacksmith's forge. Her white hair was long and straggly and matted in several places. He immediately prostrated before her. "Forgive me, great one. I did not intend to interrupt your dinner."

"Dinner?" she puzzled. "Oh, you mean the child! This is

not my dinner." A grotesquely distended arm detached from the blob of flesh and reached across the length of the cabin to caress the back of the child's head. Her hand was nearly as long as the toddler was tall. "Don't be rude, Yhtill. Say hello to the spawn of Rasputin."

The boy detached from the dangling breast and turned his head to greet their guest. "Hello, Mr. Rasputin," he said politely, mangling a few syllables as young children often do. He had seven eyes: three pairs stacked upon each other and a single, large, baleful, coal-red one in the center of his distended forehead. Each pair displayed a different emotion the boy felt in that moment—curiosity, discernment, hunger—but it was the center eye that drew the Siberian's full attention. It conveyed nothing and there was no escaping it.

"The three-souled child has been born?" Rasputin gasped.

Baba Yaga's black mouth twisted into a smile. "As promised, I have a son." She pushed against the corners of the hut and gathered her flesh into the center. It melted and reformed into a skinny, hunched-over, old woman dressed in peasant rags. Her face shrank down to normal size as she wrapped her hair into a bun. Then, she scooped up Yhtill in one arm and held him on her hip. The little one kissed her cheek and buried his head between her shoulder and neck. All of his eyes closed in contentment except for the seventh. The seventh never closed. It saw everything.

"Then the end times are coming," Rasputin said somberly.

She waved a corrective finger toward him. "No, the time of the new beginning approaches. These realms are but eggs and all eggs break for their intended purpose. His will has been made incarnate through my labor, and the faithful will be elevated to their rightful place."

"His will be done," Rasputin intoned and bowed deeply to the child cuddled against the crone. When he rose out of it, she was suddenly standing a mere foot away. Her emblazed gaze seared into him.

"What is it you seek?" she asked, tilting her head. No one visited without wanting something from her and it had been a long time since he had sought her out. He was alone, so it could not be another protégé to baptize.

"My son…I had long assumed him dead, but recent events give me hope he has returned. I very much want to find him, but he is lost to me, and there is no one greater than you who I could ask for assistance," he explained, even though he hated to admit his limitations.

Still cradling Yhtill, she paced around the Siberian, sniffing. He'd been one of the best students she'd ever had—even better than his grandfather, who had been far too distracted by ridiculous worldly matters. Unlike Grigori, this Rasputin did not waver in his dedication once he understood their master's plan. He did whatever was needed without hesitation. He was a rare human: one valuable enough to assist.

"This I will do for you," she said and waved for him to

follow her outside. She whispered to the hut, but he could not hear her exact words. The izba shivered at her coaxing and rose upon its spindly legs, revealing a massive egg where it had sat. As the hut stalked away through the trees, she tapped the egg with one of her iron-hard talons. Cracks and splits cascaded across the shell until it shattered into hundreds of small white shards. Within was a giant mortar and pestle. She climbed inside with Yhtill and beckoned Rasputin to join her.

"You know where my Yanchik is?" Rasputin asked in disbelief. Over the years, he'd tried numerous spells, rituals, divinations, and mortifications to no avail and it dumbfounded him to think she was already prepared to travel.

"I know where all my students are at all times forever and ever," she answered with a wry smile as she settled her child to one side and took hold of the pestle. "Did you think the blood that ties you to me holds no power over you?" Rasputin remembered the bilious taste of her blood in his mouth during his initiation ritual, how he'd suckled the vein like Yhtill on her breast. He climbed in and took a seat next to the babe.

With everyone inside, she whispered to the mortar until it lifted off the ground and ascended over the canopy that surrounded them. It tilted slightly as it accelerated, slowing gaining speed. As they raced over the endless wood, Rasputin struggled to breathe in the frigid air. Yhtill, however, didn't seem bothered by it.

When Baba Yaga noticed Rasputin's discomfort, she

whispered to the mortar again. The wind ceased and the pestle blasted warm air onto the Siberian. They flew in silence so long that he found it difficult to stay awake. He attributed it to the gentle rhythm of the mortar's flight and the blanket of warmth that covered him, but he couldn't discount the possibility that she had whispered once more to the mortar as it lulled him to sleep.

Chapter Eleven

Buttercrambe Hall, Yorkshire, UK
8th of March, 3:15 p.m. (GMT)

Wilson switched his windshield wipers on as the dark skies again made good on their threat of rain. The drizzle fell in that in-between zone: just enough to impede vision but not enough to keep the wipers on permanently. As soon as the rubber squeaked against the glass, he shut them off and the cycle continued a few minutes later for the entire drive to Buttercrambe Hall.

The jewel of the Leek's three-hundred-acre holding looked quite small from far off. The gate was closed, forcing him to roll down his window and press the button for the intercom for entry onto the estate. As he drove his rental car down the long blacktop, he noted the decorations and tents still on the lawn from yesterday's garden party and the *sable, three unicorns rampant or* flag at half-mast for their fallen matriarch. He pulled into the back entrance where three men dressed in white shirts and black suits were waiting for him under the grand porte-cochère.

Wilson recognized the eldest as the family's faithful butler

Taylor, who stepped forward. "Welcome back to Buttercrambe Hall, Mr. Wilson."

"Thank you, Taylor," Wilson responded as he grabbed his Korchmar Monroe attaché out of the passenger seat. The house servant retrieved Wilson's luggage and would see that it was waiting for him in his room while the valet took the wheel to park the car in the distant garage, although Wilson was well aware that Taylor would not approve of the North American use of the job description. In Britain, valets were a gentleman's gentleman and chauffeurs took care of the cars.

"It's a nasty business, even worse than what befell Master Asher—may his soul rest in peace," Taylor quickly added. Wilson took this slight indiscretion as a sign of just how worried the butler was. No one knew the ins and outs of a family like the help, who were both omnipresent and invisible.

"I'll do what I can," Wilson reassured him. "Are any of the party attendees still here?"

Taylor shook his head. "The last of them left this morning. Just the immediate family remains," by which he meant the Durand Leeks as well as the resident FitzAlan Leeks and Vries Leeks—minus Roos, who had moved on to study at Cambridge. He opened the double doors covered with a man-sized metal shield emblazed with the Leek coat of arms.

Before crossing the threshold, Wilson summoned his will. *Think, think, think...* He reached out to touch what should have been the perimeter of the wards that protected the monumental building and its immediate surroundings but found nothing there—confirmation that the MEMP had been strong enough to fry them. While not sophisticated or modern, they had been stalwart and sturdy. Now, they were ashes. He couldn't even discern a husk of the once-standing fortifications.

Taylor cleared his throat. "Lord Leek is waiting for you in his study."

Wilson nodded and stepped to. "Of course, lead the way."

Buttercrambe Hall had not changed much since his last visit, which was the point of such a grand edifice: to project a sense of permanence regardless the changing times. When repairs were needed—and they constantly were, given the Hall's size and complexity—they were done in such a way to go unnoticed so the illusion was maintained. Time may move on, but Buttercrambe Hall abides.

As Taylor led him through the house, he made a mental map and took inventory of what was there and compared it to what he remembered. The Salt Mine's files on the Leek family had grown leaps and bounds after Wilson's first visit. On top of his personal observations, a series of listening devices had been placed in strategic locations to capture the Leeks' private conversations. The Mine had acquired roughly four months of transmissions before the batteries died and Wilson came with a new set should the opportunity present itself again.

Raised voices—one female and one male—coming from the closed study door suggested Marmaduke Leek was not alone. The tone was far from civil and Wilson strained to hear what was being said.

"She's practically the same age as Asher, Dad!"

"She's still my wife and your stepmother…show her some respect."

"You don't need me here. Granny's dead and you have a new family to play lord of the manor with. Just let me go back to school," the female voice pleaded.

"You are my daughter. This is your home. This is where you belong in times of crisis."

Just then, the door flew open. "This isn't a home. It's a mausoleum!" Millicent Alice Tuppence Durand Leek yelled back at her father before storming out. She'd be damned if he was going to get the last word. The mild-mannered schoolgirl Wilson had remembered was now a full-fledged young woman with streaks of blue and purple in her hair, a nose piercing, and a lot of eye makeup. Her face was flush from the confrontation and her perfectly lined lips pursed when she saw him. "Oh, it's you…must be here about Granny. Funny how you were nowhere to be seen when *my* mom died." Her steps echoed through the house as she stomped all the way back to her room.

Marmaduke smoothed back his blond hair and rose to greet his visitor. His blue eyes were sunken and tired, but he put a weak smile on his thin lips. "Mr. Wilson, so good of you to come. You must excuse Millie. She's distraught. Mother's death has rattled us all. Taylor, could you find Ferris? Perhaps he can talk some sense into her."

"Yes, milord," he replied with a slight bow and took his leave now that he had deposited Wilson where he should be.

Marmaduke closed the study door and motioned for Wilson to take a seat. "Can I offer you a drink?"

Wilson set his attaché down and unbuttoned his jacket before sitting in a worn leather chair. The patina of the dark green leather was a testament to its age and quality to have stood the test of time. "No, thank you, but don't let that stop you from having one."

"I think I will." Marmaduke went to the sideboard and poured himself a whisky. "Listen, I want to clear the air and start fresh. I know I objected to your investigation of Asher's death, but I see now it was necessary. I hope there are no hard feelings about what happened before."

You mean when you had the help pack my things and kicked me out the second your mother had a heart attack? the petty part of Wilson chimed in, but he set it aside. "Water under the bridge. Now, I understand the attack happened yesterday and you were the one that inadvertently triggered the MEMP, thinking it was a suicide note."

"That's what's great about you Yanks—straight to business." Marmaduke took a sip from his glass before answering. "That's correct. It was sitting on my mother's dressing table with my name on it. The MEMP went off as soon as I opened it."

"Do you still have it?"

Marmaduke nodded. "I removed it before the police arrived, but I put it back once they were gone—to preserve the scene. I thought we'd start with that and see if you can find anything," he alluded to his current lack of magical ability.

"I will inspect it, of course, but I doubt I'll find anything through magical means. On my way in, I noticed the wards around the house are completely obliterated. If that was from the MEMP, it's unlikely that anything inside the house was spared," Wilson explained.

Marmaduke made a fist and slammed it down on the desk. "Damn SES!"

"We don't know that they are responsible, but if we find that they are, there will be consequences. As you know, MEMPs are a forbidden magic," Wilson said neutrally.

Marmaduke scoffed. "Who else could it be?!"

"Any number of people or groups: someone with a grudge against your family or the Dawn Club, someone within the Club that wants to assume power. It could even be a feint for a robbery—a chance to steal something enchanted after substituting it with a dud that won't be suspect when everything here has been hit with the MEMP," Wilson threw out options. "The point is, if we narrow the investigation at this stage, it increases the likelihood that whoever did it will get away with it, and neither of us want that."

Marmaduke slumped in his chair. He hadn't even considered that one of his guests could have set it up. When his mother failed to make her entrance, they just had to go far enough to be out of its radius and return after the fact, pretending to be a victim to the very bomb they had created. If the culprit was supposed to be at the Hall, no one would bat an eye if they were inside the house or out on the grounds. After he'd discovered his mother's body, it seemed reasonable for everyone to leave Buttercrambe Hall in haste, but what if one of them was the guilty party fleeing the scene of the crime?

He tried to remember if anyone had been acting strangely or if he'd seen someone out of place, but it was impossible to know who was where at all times. There were so many people here for the meeting, and now that they had all gone home, there would be no easy way for the Salt Mine agent to verify if they had really been affected. The idea of one of his peers laughing at him as he set off the weapon that robbed his family of their arcane abilities and enchanted possessions raised his ire. "What kind of justice can we hope to have for this heinous attack?"

"It depends on what is found during the investigation and the severity of the MEMP. In past cases, there has been financial restitution for damages, prison sentences for the guilty, loss of employment and blacklisting for complicity. In extreme cases, entire agencies and groups have also been added to enemy-action lists by the various bodies around the world. Everyone takes forbidden magic seriously."

Marmaduke's eyebrow raised. "A magical war?"

Wilson tilted his head and slightly shrugged his shoulders. "More like a magical *cold* war. Everything remains as discreet as possible but flagging an agency as rogue allows everyone else to attack it from all sides. The threat of that is usually enough to convince the organization to agree to other far less-drastic corrective measures."

The talk of punishment put Marmaduke in better spirits. "Okay, what would you like to see first?"

"Let's start with your mother's room and the trigger note. Then I'd like to walk the grounds to get an idea of the MEMP's radius. I'd also like to take a look at the security footage—more than likely it captured whoever shot your mother," Wilson enumerated his plan.

Marmaduke's face soured. "Ah, about that. I'm afraid there's nothing to see. Basil and I had much the same thought after we had the family meeting and decided there was no way Mother killed herself. When we went to take a look for ourselves, we found the system down and yesterday's CD missing from the rack."

Wilson leaned forward—that had not been in his briefing. "When was that?"

"Yesterday evening after the police had left."

"And you didn't think to mention that sooner?" Wilson questioned him.

"You were already on your way. Is it really that important?" he deflected.

Wilson wanted to shake the tall man about the shoulders and scream, "Of course it's important! It raises the whole caliber of the operation. Whoever did this knew enough about your security to cover their tracks and gives us another data point in the timeline!" But he didn't. There was no need to kick a man when he was down.

Instead, Wilson just said, "Yes," calmly. "We should definitely go there after we finish in Cordelia's room." He rose and picked up his attaché while Marmaduke tipped his tumbler to finish his drink.

Chapter Twelve

Buttercrambe Hall, Yorkshire, UK
8th of March, 3:53 p.m. (GMT)

Marmaduke led the way to his mother's bedroom, which was actually a suite with a connected bathroom. The front room, which Wilson knew to be called the dressing room, thanks to Taylor, was where she'd been shot. "She was all dressed for the party, sitting in her favorite chair. I've tried to leave everything as it was and put the note back where I found it after the police left," he informed Wilson. He stayed by the door while Wilson took a closer look.

The body had been removed but the cleaners had yet to come. Based on the blood pooled on the carpet and upholstery and the matter splattered on the wall, Cordelia had been sitting in the armchair when a bullet passed through one temple and out the other. The coroner's initial examination found gunshot residue on her hands, but that didn't mean she pulled the trigger herself. The instinct for self-preservation went deep, making it challenging to arcanely compel someone to kill themselves. It was much easier to magically incapacitate them and stage a fatal self-inflicted wound. Under normal circumstances, he would have visited the morgue and obtained a magical signature via salt-casting, but her body was at ground zero of an MEMP. Any residual magic would have burned away.

He ran his will over the tri-folded piece of paper propped up against a hat on the dressing table addressed to "My dearest Daunty." The MEMP should have stripped it of enchantment, but it was better to be safe than sorry. When he found it magically inert, he donned disposable gloves before handling it. He didn't hold out much hope for finding forensic evidence but he came prepared to get lucky.

The paper had a good heft in the hand and the black ink stood out against the light ecru of the stationery. Below Cordelia's custom header was a single word: *Boom*. He held the sheet up to the window to see if there was a hidden message written in lemon juice, mineral spirits, or brake fluid, but only found a watermark: a feather and a globe.

"Do you recognize this as her handwriting and letter stock?" he asked Marmaduke.

"The stationery is authentic. We've employed Symthson for our personal stationery for generations. The writing looks like hers, but Mother didn't write the note," he said emphatically. "She always used a fountain pen filled with gold ink for personal correspondences. The only time she used black was for business affairs. Government documents were always blue."

"And it was no secret that she called you Daunty," Wilson added. He always found British nicknames silly, but he couldn't think of the better one for such a trainwreck of a name. "Do you know where she kept her writing paraphernalia?"

Marmaduke pointed at her writing cabinet. The inside was divided by vertical panels and drawers of various sizes. Wilson found several pots of J Herbin's *Ambre de Birmanie* in one drawer. "The ink is also bespoke. It contains the finest granules of real gold. She did that so you could never mistake her ink for the mass-produced ink," Marmaduke explained.

Wilson poked around and found an unsealed letter penned in gold ink written to someone named Celia complaining about the poor quality of the latest repair on the south wall—confirmation of Marmaduke's theory. He was about to return the letter to its envelope when the header caught his eye. He placed it side by side with the trigger note: they were definitely different. "Are these both your mother's stationery?"

Marmaduke leaned in. "Yes, but this one's older," he said, pointing to the MEMP's trigger. "Mother had the font changed and enlarged a while back. She said it was a stylistic choice but we all knew it was because of her eyesight. She never did like to wear her readers."

"How long ago was this?"

"Maybe ten years ago?" He took a stab in the dark. "She made quite a kerfuffle over it."

"Would she have kept the old stationery?"

He shook his head. "It would have been destroyed as soon as the new one arrived. She was quite particular about these things."

Wilson narrowed it down to two possibilities: either someone snatched this at least ten years ago, or whoever was supposed to destroy the old stock did not because the watermarks matched. "I need to know the exact date when she changed her stationery as well as the time before."

Marmaduke nodded gravely—clearly, whoever killed his mother had history with her and proximity to her personal possessions in the past. "I'll check if we have records on that. If we don't, I'm sure Symthson will."

"Who was the last person to see your mother alive?" Wilson moved on with his questions.

"Taylor asked if she wanted tea at 2:30. She declined."

"And you found her a few minutes after 4:00?"

"That's right. She made her entrance at 4:01 and I came up when she didn't come out."

That piqued Wilson's interest. "That's an oddly specific time. Was this something she normally did?"

"The time of her birth," Marmaduke explained. "It's something she did ever since she became Ipsissimus."

"So, it's something everyone knew about—all the staff and attendees?"

"Yes, I suppose so," Marmaduke confirmed, even though he was uncomfortable with what it implied.

"Interesting. What about the Beretta 9000 found next to her…was it one of the family's firearms?"

"No, we don't keep any pistols on the premises. All of ours are shotguns and rifles. And locked in the gun safe."

"Did anyone inside the house hear the shot...perhaps one of the staff?"

"No one said anything. Perhaps the shooter used a silencer and took it with them?" Marmaduke suggested.

"Suppressors only reduce the noise. Gunfire is still pretty loud even when they're on," Wilson corrected a common misconception.

"It must have been sometime when the band was playing," Marmaduke concluded.

"When did they start?"

"3:30 on the dot."

Wilson made a note of the time. There were ninety minutes unaccounted for. In that time, someone came into Cordelia's room, likely incapacitated her—an accomplished practitioner—and set the stage for her suicide, waited for the band to play to do the deed, and then got far enough away to avoid getting caught in the MEMP. It was possible they shot her sooner and used some sort of magic to cover up the noise to give them more time to get away, but they still had to clear the house and the lawn at the very least. It was one hell of a tight window. Whoever did this had a lot of operational awareness of the target and the property, and possibly had inside help as well.

Wilson pulled out a plastic bag. "If it's all right with you,

I'd like to send the trigger note to our lab to be analyzed."

"Take it," Marmaduke said with a dismissive wave of his hand. "It's brought nothing but misery."

With the note secured in his attaché, Wilson took off his glove and motioned toward the door. "Let's see the security room."

He was already quite familiar with Buttercrambe Hall's security: a rudimentary CCTV system that had been installed to record to VCR and upgraded to CDs at some point in the distant past. The system recorded in local memory in fifteen-minute bursts before writing it to one of the CDs in the tower. One of the servants changed the disks every day and the Leeks kept a rolling year's worth of recordings for insurance purposes.

Overall, it was entirely antiquated and pathetically weak. Its strong points focused on the upper-story library that contained a Shakespeare's First Folio and the antechamber leading to the Leek family arcane vault. Unfortunately, its efficacy was undercut by the decision to run parallel systems that did not communicate with each other instead of upgrading the whole system.

The security room was a glorified walk-in closet. There was a desk with a bank of eight small screens, a tablet, and a computer approaching two decades old. A thick cable attached a CD read/write tower with fourteen slots to the computer, and a CD storage cabinet took up the majority of one wall. He immediately recognized the brick-sized piece of electronica on top of the desk beside the computer: an EMP. It was currently unplugged but well within reach of the lone surge protector that serviced all of the devices in the room.

"Who unplugged it?" Wilson asked as he pulled out a fresh pair of gloves.

"Basil did—thought maybe everything would come back online once he did."

Wilson put a bio to the name: Basil Grant Thomas Vries Leek, age thirty-seven, another resident of Buttercrambe Hall from the Vries Leek branch of the family. He was the tall, dark, and handsome public face of the Leek family who made appearances at country fetes and handed out ribbons at community competitions. "When did you and Basil find it like this?"

"A little after six," Marmaduke said after some thought. So much had happened yesterday, it was all a blur. "It didn't seem to affect any of the other electrics in the house."

Wilson bent down to visually follow the connections from all angles. "That's because this would have generated a small, localized EMP—devices would have to be close to be zapped." He picked it up and examined it. It looked field-made by a naïve but knowledgeable hand. The capacitor was big but the wiring and soldering lacked the polish of practiced precision. Whoever did it also knew about old tech—the CDs contained optical, not electronic, data and were immune to EMPs—so they knew they'd have to take the most-recent recording to fully cover their tracks.

Then a thought occurred to him: what if the EMP wasn't just to get away with both murder and setting up the MEMP? "Have you done an inventory of your valuables since your mother's death?" Wilson asked Marmaduke as he placed the EMP in a separate bag for processing.

The question puzzled Marmaduke. "Pardon?"

"I find it a little odd that the MEMP was such a big explosion while the EMP that disabled the security system was so discrete. Buttercrambe Hall contains many valuable things—not all of them enchanted in nature—and there were a lot of people in and out of here yesterday," Wilson explained his thought process.

A light went off behind Marmaduke's eyes as it dawned on him that the system could have been down all day yesterday, perhaps even before his mother had been shot. "Good God… the First Folio!"

Chapter Thirteen

Buttercrambe Hall, Yorkshire, UK
8th of March, 4:31 p.m. (GMT)

Buttercrambe Hall's second-floor library was much grander than the aspirational overgrown studies people generously called libraries. The walls were lined with nine rows of bookshelves topped with various bronze and marble busts. There were only four breaks in the shelving where the walls weren't covered in books: two for windows, one for a larger than life-sized painting of one of the early Leeks, and one that housed the exquisite Regency-era library ladder. There were two single-person reading tables near the windows to take advantage of the natural light. It was the stuff of bibliophilic dreams.

The majority of the books were bound in old, soft-brown leather, and even the modern titles tended to be leather-bound collections. The exception to the rule was a shelf dedicated to first editions from such luminaries as Austen, Dickens, Byron, Kipling, Shelley, Blake, and of course, the sisters Brontë. While many of those tomes were valuable in their own right, the priceless books were held in a temperature-controlled display case situated between the library's two entrances. Marmaduke exhaled in relief when he saw the First Folio where it was supposed to be: nestled between a Gutenberg Bible and Caxton's second illustrated edition of Chaucer's Canterbury Tales.

"You need to get a new security system up and running as quickly as possible," Wilson suggested. "Until then, best to move prized possessions into the various safes hidden throughout the house, but not the obvious ones like the one behind that gentleman," he said, pointing to the portrait of the Leek ancestor.

The color drained from Marmaduke's face.

"Don't worry. It's only obvious to me because it's my job to notice these things," Wilson reassured him. "Use the ones in your personal quarters if you must. Better yet, if someone in your family was wise enough to put in a priest hole in the past, use that. They are harder to spot because they were built centuries ago and aren't in line with modern concepts of space and concealment. They are easy to overlook, even for professionals."

"All that can be arranged." Marmaduke nodded at the sound advice. The security system was a requirement for the insurance company and he worried that anything stolen while it was down might not be covered by the policy.

"It would also be a good idea to see if anything is missing from the vault," Wilson added.

"I don't see much point in that. Everything in there was hit by the MEMP, and insurance doesn't cover disenchantment,"

Marmaduke objected. Wilson let the matter drop but noted the resistance.

"It's your call. Unless there is anything else you'd like to show me in the house, I'd like to make the most of what daylight is left to walk the grounds."

"Do you require an escort?" Marmaduke offered.

That's the difference between mother and son—Cordelia would have assigned me one while Marmaduke asked, Wilson observed as he shook his head. "No, just a sturdy umbrella, please." With a tug of a rope, Marmaduke summoned a member of the staff to assist Wilson before returning to his office to see to the restoration of the security system.

The Leeks had placed Wilson in the same room as before, and he welcomed the serendipity. It would allow him to leisurely swap out batteries in the transmitter he'd hidden in the box springs on his last visit. His luggage had been brought in from the car and was waiting for him on a luggage rack. He changed into clothing more suitable for the outdoors. He retrieved his Glock 24, double-checked that it was still loaded with banishment bullets, and slipped it into his shoulder holster. In his pockets, he tucked his saltcaster and hag stone. While a MEMP shorted out magic, it didn't poison a place for magic to happen. Wilson's arcane arsenal would work as normal; it just required a little lateral thinking on how to apply it.

If metaphysical reality was a still lake, using magic to glean information of what happened was looking at the reflection on its surface. Setting off an MEMP was like hucking a rock into that lake. It created a moment in time that could never be reflected clearly again. He could, however, determine how far the energy from the MEMP went.

He donned a light jacket to conceal his weapon and by the time he was ready to set off, a wide, vented golf umbrella was waiting for him outside the door. His first stop was the lawn. The rain had done a number on the decorations and the tents seemed particularly empty with all the furniture there but none of the people. There was something sullen about event spaces after the party was over but before everything had been cleared. It reminded him of Bourbon Street early Sunday morning before the street cleaners had a chance to hose everything down, or when the fair had closed but hadn't left town. Along the perimeter were a series of citronella torches, one every twenty feet, ostensibly to keep mosquitos at bay, but the enchanted ones owned by the Leek family performed that magically. They were also used to extend the Hall's wards to their outdoor entertainment area.

He stood at the top of the lawn and peered through the hag stone, starting his mental count as soon as his eye lined up with the naturally bored hole of the smooth stone. *One Mississippi… two Mississippi…three Mississippi….* The color drained from the world and not a single torch glowed: the MEMP had penetrated the entire garden party.

He walked beyond the last torch to a gazebo overlooking a small fish pond. It was a scenic spot to get out of the rain or catch some shade on hot, sunny days. Like many of the outdoor structures, its wood had been enchanted to resist rot, termites, and woodworm. Instead of the hag stone, this time he pulled out his vape pen and lined up the notches before bringing it to his lips and blowing salt out the sigiled chamber. He continued to pantomime vaping while he waited for a result. To anyone watching, it looked like he was simply taking a nicotine break.

When the grains shifted into a magical signature, he mentally marked the gazebo as unaffected. It was quite a distance from the party on the lawn, and he looked for something in between that might be enchanted to refine his estimation of the MEMP's radius. He backtracked to a different side of the house where the gardens were located as well as a tool shed, hot house, and open fields. The English were quite fond of their horticulture, and magical families often used minor magics to prepare the soil and ensure a good harvest. The formal, ornamental gardens were closer to the house and definitely affected, but the fields extended farther out. There was a chance some of them were spared.

Since he needed to cover a lot of ground again, he put the hag stone to his eye and was immediately drawn to a bright spot in a distant field: a line of demarcation where the MEMP's energy had petered out. He trudged into the muddy field whose overwinter crop had recently been turned under. When he was close, he used the hag stone a third and final time to precisely pin down its location and added a geopin on his phone. Using Cordelia's room as the epicenter, he now had the MEMP's radius, which could be used to estimate the magnitude of the damage—not by him, of course, but by the specialists in the Salt Mine's sixth floor. Harold Weber and Hans Lundqvist had refined the science of magical energy using the data acquired from the Drill Hall of the Detroit Masonic Lodge.

After Wilson sent off the coordinates, he checked the time on his phone—enough to have a word with Marmaduke before dinner. He would be able to interview everyone at the Hall this evening, but he didn't relish tracking down all ones that had already left. According to the list Marmaduke had provided the Mine, they consisted of the Dawn Club's six major families and three of the lesser ones to build up the roster. Thankfully, his brief foray onto the Leek estate had given him another idea of finding possible witnesses without having to traipse all over England. All he needed to do was convince Marmaduke to go along.

Chapter Fourteen

Buttercrambe Hall, Yorkshire, UK
8th of March, 6:20 p.m. (GMT)

Marmaduke Leek reluctantly led Wilson into Cordelia's room for a second time—not to reexamine anything inside, but to access the Leek family vault. Constructed in 1589, it was a secret basement nestled in the middle of the house, unconnected to any of the other basements. The only entrance was through a locked door in the largest bedroom in the Hall: Cordelia's. Under normal circumstances, he would never have allowed a stranger entry, but these were unusual times and Wilson's argument for why he needed access had been persuasive.

The vault contained the Leek's servant roster which included supernatural creatures, the bulk of which were bound into service by John Leek, one of the family's greatest practitioners who'd died over a hundred years ago. These faeries had been at the Hall for generations of Leeks and many a Dawn Club meeting. They would know the faces of family, staff, and repeat visitors. Wilson hoped that one of them saw something unusual.

Unfortunately, the faeries were no longer bound to Buttercrambe Hall. The MEMP would have broken the binding that kept them and banished them back to their native realms. Lucky for the Leeks, Wilson was a master summoner. If he knew their true names, he could summon them for questioning. According to family lore, each and every one of their true names was somewhere in the Leek family ledger.

Removing it from the vault was out of the question and he didn't feel comfortable taking digital pictures of the required pages. Those could be circulated with far too much ease. That only left him one course of action: bring Wilson to it. He told the disapproving voice in his head—which sounded remarkably like his mother's—that this was necessary. Plus, he really should check to make sure nothing had been stolen. The items in the vault were still antiques and held some value, albeit a fraction of what it used to be when they were enchanted.

He said nothing as he retrieved an eight-inch wrought iron key from a false-bottomed drawer of his late mother's writing desk and approached a large tapestry of a woman standing in a paddock holding a black flag on a pole. Around her pranced three golden unicorns. It looked medieval in style, but Wilson suspected it was significantly more modern than that and merely emulated the aesthetic. Marmaduke pulled the tapestry to one side and revealed a locked door. With a turn of the key, it opened to a stone spiral staircase going down.

The passage was barely big enough for a single person. Marmaduke, who was tall like his mother had been, had to crouch down to avoid hitting his head. Wilson had no difficulties at 5'5". They went in single file, with Marmaduke in the lead holding a large flashlight in hand. The way had previously been magically lit but now they had to rely on technology for illumination. Wilson closed the door behind them and recognized the runes and sigils engraved on it—one of which was an alarm that alerted the keeper of the wards whenever the door was opened. Being thorough, he ran his will over them and found nothing as expected.

The stairs went down the entire height of the house. The walls were roughly worked, but the stairs themselves were hewn smooth. It was one of two sections of the original house that had survived the blaze of 1786 and the only part unscathed due to magical protections against fire—the greatest natural risk at the time. Even the Great Chamber—exceptional example of late Elizabethan interior design that it was—had required repairs after the conflagration.

The stairwell ended at a thick reinforced iron door that opened away from them. Edged by stone, its hinges were hidden along with the gaps around its perimeter, leaving no space for a pry bar to gain purchase. The same key that unlocked the door behind the tapestry fit the lock. Marmaduke forcefully pushed it open. A red brick prominently stamped "Whitaker Elland RD Leeds" announced that the barrel-vaulted stone antechamber had been bricked and mortared sometime in the industrial period. Inset in the masonry were runes against all manner of magical intrusion made of yellow brick. Stripped of their metaphysical power, they were now mere decoration against the red ones. The setup reminded Wilson of a miniature version of the Mine's magical gauntlet he always passed through after field work.

Beyond the door on the other side of the antechamber was the vault proper. It was a rather primitive storage facility compared to the grandeur of the rest of Buttercrambe Hall: two long rows of shelves made of rough-hewn oak planks and stacked bricks on either side of the walkway. The same wards in the antechamber were repeated on the walls, only these were etched into the stone and inlaid with pure gold.

Wilson was surprised at the paucity of items. On the far end of the vault were a half dozen armor stands holding various bits from the Tudor and Stuart periods. There was also an array of weaponry—daggers, hammers, swords, pole-arms, and a few early firearms—but none of the strange and unusual treasures he'd expected to find in the vault of such an old and established magical family. "Anything missing?" he asked.

"No, it's as it was when last I looked," Marmaduke replied, unfazed by the gaps on the shelves where things once sat but no longer did.

"If I may be so bold," Wilson prefaced deferentially as he ran his fingers along a recent dust line, "where's the rest of it?"

"Divested in exchange for raw capital," he answered in financial jargon. "In light of the most recent push for government oversight of magical affairs," he added to ensure no one got the impression the Leeks were hard up for cash. "This isn't the first time talks of something like the Secret Esoteric Service came up, but the Dawn Club always had the clout to squash it before it went anywhere. The last big flare up was in the '70s. We had Maggie at the helm then and enough support in the government to defeat it. Sadly, we are not as numerous as we once were, and the latest string of prime ministers are some of the worst bunch of venal, petty, short-term thinkers England has ever had. One after another, like tramps climbing out of a clown car," Marmaduke said bitterly. He tamped down his emotions and returned to his narrative. "Mother caught wind of a scheme to create registration, taxation, and confiscation programs of enchanted paraphernalia in this latest itineration and got ahead of it all."

Wilson nodded in comprehension. "She hedged her bets in case it actually came to fruition. Fiscal capital can always be sheltered through the old, familiar ways. The government won't come after that."

Marmaduke smiled. "My mother was a difficult woman, but she rarely led us down the wrong path. The divestment started off slowly about decade ago but she picked up the pace after Asher's death, leaving us with what you see here."

"Not a lot of demand for swords that don't lose their edge

or armor that doesn't rust?" Wilson guessed.

Marmaduke let out a cynical laugh. "They don't even have that going for them now, I suppose. It appears Mother had the right of it one final time. Had she delayed, our losses would have been much greater." He went to a small stack of books and pulled out the one labeled "Ledger" in silver-embossed letters along its two-inch-thick spine. "I believe what you are looking for is in here."

Marmaduke conveyed the book to a table and chair set off to one side. He positioned the flashlight to provide as much illumination to the pages as possible. Although the artificial light was much brighter, he thought it lacked the warmth and charm of the magical ones that used to be active. He placed the book on a stand and reverently opened it. He started at the beginning and cursed when he saw the ornate round-hand cursive that sprawled across the page in a swirl of delicate ink— he knew of the book's existence, but this was the first time he'd actually cracked it open.

"I spend a lot of time reading old writing. Would you like me to try?" Wilson tactfully offered.

"It's my family's history. I should be the one to read it," Marmaduke insisted. "I don't see much handwriting beyond a thank you note these days. Everything's digital or printed out, but it's like riding a bike. Just give me a second to get used to it. I'll be ship-shape in no time."

"Of course," Wilson conceded to his host's pride and

made no mention of his mixed metaphor. While Marmaduke muddled through the first page, Wilson pulled out a small travel flashlight from his pocket—he always carried his own light source—and scanned the remaining books for anything on the ALWAYS RETRIEVE list.

The early pages were a mix of inventories, wage recordings, purchases and sales, and brief histories of the year starting in the Year of Our Lord 1513. There was a lot of estate to manage—even then, Buttercrambe Hall was the largest of the Leek holdings—and every entry had to be read to find the names of the oathbound faeries the family had collected over time. Each time a new recorder took the helm, the penmanship changed, sometimes for the worse, sometimes for the better.

In 1715, all the entries regarding the old Buttercrambe Hall ceased and the ledger focused primarily on Sugarside-on-Sandy, a sugar plantation run by Sir Thomas Leek. Located in Jamaica not far from Kingston, it consisted of two thousand acres along the west bank of the Sandy River. Marmaduke ran his eyes down the extensive slave list: each human reduced to a brief description and the name assigned to them by Sir Thomas with births, deaths, purchases, and sales noted in much the same fashion as the other chattel of the estate.

He quickly flipped through the next one hundred years spent in Jamaica and resumed the hunt for true names once the ledger returned to English matters at Buttercrambe Hall. He eventually found the list of fae servants in the late 1800s into the early twentieth century. Unfortunately, they were much the same as the list of slaves kept in Jamaica: a brief description and the name given to them by John Leek. There were no true names. There wasn't even a record of their public names—the names they widely used amongst themselves. Every fae had at least one such public name and it wasn't uncommon for them to have several, much like people go by different nicknames depending on their company. While it conferred no power over them like a true name, a summoner could work with it because a public name identified an individual faerie from others of their kind. Its omission struck Wilson as callous, but that was in keeping with what he knew of the Leeks, past and present.

"I don't understand," a confused Marmaduke uttered under his breath. "Mother said they were in here."

Wilson seized the opportunity to take a closer look over Marmaduke's shoulder and found a familiar name among the two dozen fae once bound to Leek service: Dirt Feather. That was the winged maker he'd liberated on his first visit to Buttercrambe Hall in exchange for placing the bugs around the house, unbeknownst to any of the Leeks. "Perhaps that's what she was told and she never had reason to look it up herself," he offered a plausible explanation as he jotted down the names on a piece of paper. "If it's any consolation, it's possible John Leek never knew their true names and was a better practitioner than previously thought." Two dozen bindings was ambitious; as a fellow summoner, he could appreciate how impressive a feat it was, particularly if John Leek didn't have their public or true names.

The comment was cold comfort to Marmaduke and it rubbed salt in the wound that was the theft of his own ability to practice magic. The lack of true names was the proverbial straw that broke the camel's back—the small insult that came on the heels of a string of devastating losses that had befallen him in less than thirty-six hours. To his immediate regret, he slammed the ledger shut. The enchantments that had preserved the old tome and kept the silverfish at bay were now gone and if the old books were to last, he had to be a better steward than he was being right now. Apologetically, he gently put the ledger back where he'd found it. "Well, that's that. I suppose you'll have to do this the hard way."

"Not necessarily. There is a chance I can summon one of the fae on the list, even without a true name or a public name."

Marmaduke made no effort to suppress his shock. "Really?"

Wilson glossed over his host's assumption that he was not an accomplished practitioner. "I'll still proceed with interviewing everyone at the Hall today, but it's certainly worth a try tomorrow. Do you have a summoning chamber?"

Marmaduke shook his head, "No, but we should have whatever accoutrements you require and you'll have your pick of the rooms in the Hall."

"I'll make a list, but outdoors would be better for summoning fae," Wilson accepted Marmaduke's offer even though he traveled with everything he needed for such a simple summoning.

"We should be going if you want to squeeze in a few interviews before dinner."

The mention of a Leek family dinner soured his stomach. He couldn't imagine what a zoo it would be without Cordelia to keep everyone in line. He mustered up some enthusiasm before he spoke, "Sounds good. You know, this isn't a bad place to move your valuables to until the security system is back online. There's only one way in, it's well-concealed, and no modern thief would be prepared to deal with such a heavy lock. I'm assuming that's the only key?"

Marmaduke hesitated to reveal any more of their secrets to an outsider but eventually answered in the affirmative. "It is."

"Then your possessions will be safer here than in any standard home safe as long as you secure the key." *And there's plenty of space on the shelves*, he added just to himself.

Chapter Fifteen

Buttercrambe Hall, Yorkshire, UK
8th of March, 10:49 p.m. (GMT)

Wilson wearily entered his room and closed the door behind him. He was finally alone and he savored the sound of silence. He replayed the evening as he partially undressed and hung his suit jacket and tie in the room's Victorian walnut double-door wardrobe. Dinner had been a veritable banquet as the chef repurposed the mountain of food that had been designated to feed a houseful of guests. All extra groceries ordered for the Dawn Club's meeting had been canceled, but there was nothing to be done about what had already been delivered.

The meal had passed without incident and Marmaduke's new wife did most of the talking. Mary was a pretty thing and the bloom of youth made up for what she lacked in sophistication and style—something her predecessor had had in spades. It was little wonder why Marmaduke married her; she was filled to the brim with the blind hope of one with many more days ahead of them than behind.

It appeared Ferris had talked some sense into his younger

sister. Despite her previous outburst in her father's study, Millicent had managed to be civil to her new stepmother throughout the whole meal. Grant's volume had grown louder the more he drank despite Curwen's admonishments, but he did not let anything indiscreet slip in his inebriation, probably because he was so well-acquainted with that state. Basil's toast to the empty chair at the head of the table had been touching without being overly sentimental. On the whole, everyone in the family had seemed more at ease now that there was no threat of Cordelia's criticism or disapproval. She had been a demanding woman.

One by one, he'd met with the resident Leeks and house staff and went over their movements yesterday. It was tedious but necessary work that didn't pan out any leads. No one saw or heard anything out of the ordinary, and he didn't get the impression that any of them were lying or holding anything back. However, it hadn't been a complete bust: he had confirmed that all the practitioner Leeks were definitely affected by the MEMP's blast.

He examined his room for cameras and checked for microphones with his electric shaver that also acted as a non-linear junction detector. Once he'd ruled all the positives as false ones, he turned out the lights. Using the black light and infrared setting on his flashlight, he completed his routine security check before he allowed himself to fully relax. He shimmied under the bed and retrieved the transmitter he'd stashed in the box springs two years ago. After a quick battery change, it was ready to go. Now, all he had to do was place new bugs.

He checked his phone and found a message from the Salt Mine: the sixth floor had done the calculations and it wasn't looking good for the Dawn Club. Those closest to the epicenter were likely permanently unable to wield magic. He opened the attachment and saw the diagram Weber had drawn up delineating zones of impact using a familiar color-coded scheme where red was bad and green was good. Anyone inside the house and standing within the first twenty yards of the lawn were certainly toast. Those along the periphery might recover in time, but to what extent and how long it would take was anyone's guess. Weber might be on the vanguard of arcane energy transference technology, but little was known about the progression of MEMP damage on practitioners.

Wilson divided the Leeks into two categories: those definitely in the red zone and those that had a chance of recovery. There was some margin of error because while everyone had a general idea of where they were when the MEMP went off, they hadn't been able to mark exactly where they were standing. He sent a request to the Salt Mine's analysts—find and collate all pictures posted on social media from the event. Using the torches and tents as landmarks, they might be able to figure out who had a chance of recovery, which would be valuable information when he went around to interview people…not to mention all the data points it would give Weber to further his knowledge on the subject. Wilson saw little to be gained telling Marmaduke about the results tonight. Knowing sooner wouldn't change the reality: he would never practice magic again.

The next message confirmed that the fingerprint he'd lifted off the EMP was Basil Leek's, which was consistent with Marmaduke's account. Because there was a chance of fingerprints on the interior from when it was assembled, he decided to express post the EMP to the Salt Mine in the morning along with the trigger letter. He didn't hold out hope they would provide something actionable, but it wouldn't be the first time his doggedness gave him an advantage when an opponent slipped up.

He showered and readied for bed—no skulking around Buttercrambe Hall at night for him this time around. Even though the security system was down, he didn't want to risk being caught acting suspicious and he didn't have Navaratna, the true Gomeda, to render him invisible this time. It wouldn't be hard to place listening devices about the Hall during the course of his investigation. Unlike his mother, Marmaduke did not insist Wilson be constantly chaperoned. The new lord of the manor had much more pressing things to worry about than the American he'd employed.

Additionally, Wilson needed his rest for tomorrow's summonings. Fae had never been his go-to for information. He much preferred a litigious, contract-bound devil over a flighty spirit-of-the-truth faerie. All the ones bound to Leek service were lesser fae, and attracting their kind wasn't hard if the summoner knew what to use as bait. Most faeries would respond to a sweet, although some had favored offerings, like a bit of cheese for a rat rider. While his knowledge on summoning various kinds of fae was robust, he wasn't just looking for a specific type. He was looking for singular individuals and the only thing he had to find them was their slave name.

Fortunately, he had an in: Dirt Feather. He'd done the winged maker a favor by freeing it from bondage. Even though he didn't know its public or true name, there was a chance it might respond to him using the name John Leek had given it. From Dirt Feather, he could obtain the public name of the other resident fae, but even if his plan worked, it required at least two dozen summonings to speak to them all, which was a considerable expenditure of will. He didn't worry about the karmic cost—the Mine would cover the expense—but he was still the one who had to do the work. It would be tiring.

He turned on the bedside light and killed the main before donning his pajamas and climbing into bed. He pulled the blankets to his chin against the chill of a freshly washed body and the cold Yorkshire night outside. Why the rest of the world hadn't adopted forced-air heating was a mystery to him. As he lay in bed, he studied the plasterwork cornicing found in nearly every room of Buttercrambe Hall. It was an architectural detail most missed, but Wilson made of habit of looking up.

These were ornate Corinthian column tops jutting from the wall to the ceiling every two feet, giving the illusion they were loadbearing. They were bedecked with foliage, much like the ceiling rose that covered nearly half of the ceiling. Each acanthus leaf was shaped just so and his eyes followed a wisteria vine wending through the larger leaves in the centerpiece. The small bedside lamp cast long shadows across the plaster, and he fancifully imagined them as some dark part of the terrain of faerie.

As far as he knew, he was one of the few humans to have even glimpsed the Land of the Fae. When he'd freed Alberia, she'd sundered the veil between the Magh Meall and the Land of the Fae, providing him a glimpse of what lay beyond the rainbow bridge: the fabled city of Tír na nÓg, a place where no human had ever stepped. He could still hear Leader's atypical giggle as the child of Oberon and Titania broke free from her chrysalis. The immense light radiating from Alberia had seared her silhouette into his mind forever. It would have been enough to kill him had the fomoire not shielded him from its full effects.

The whole thing had been unimaginably beautiful. Every time he thought about it, he could never find the right words to do it justice, even to himself. But it had also been unimaginably terrifying. For the briefest moment, he'd experienced the power contained in the Land of the Fae, and the only thing he could compare it to was that old scene in Indiana Jones right after the

Nazis opened the Ark of the Covenant but before their faces melted off. The memory sent him shivering despite the intense heat he'd come to associate with it, and he buried himself deeper in the blankets.

It had forever altered his perception of the fae and left him wondering if they really were as terrible as the fiends of Pandemonium. There was a well-established animosity between the two realms and although he'd never fallen prey to the false dichotomy—devils and demons were monstrous and wanted to consume your soul so beautiful faeries must be good, right?—he'd never really put them on even footing.

After the raw display he'd witnessed, he wondered what chance humanity stood if the powers that resided in Tír na nÓg decided to be adversarial instead of indifferent to mortals? What if faeries were just more subtly evil and the good, helpful ones were little more than lures at the end of an anglerfish's ray fin? Was there a massive jaw poised to bite somewhere in the darkness just beyond human perception? Since being in Alberia's presence, he hadn't summoned a single fae, and when he had to go into the Magh Meall, he actively avoided them all. Now, he had to summon two dozen of them.

He switched off the table lamp and for a brief moment, the shadows disappeared into the darkness. As his eyes adjusted, he saw a new batch of shadows form from the ambient light that painted the ceiling and walls. That was the thing about shadows: they were always in the darkness that lurked in every direction, and you couldn't spot them without the light.

Chapter Sixteen

Buttercrambe Hall, Yorkshire, UK
9th of March, 10:13 a.m. (GMT)

After a hearty breakfast and a quick dash into town, Wilson began his search for a place to perform his summoning. He'd been given access to one of the estate's four-wheelers to survey Buttercrambe Hall's three hundred acres for a suitable spot. Were he not so focused on the task at hand, he would have stopped to appreciate the sullen beauty of the Yorkshire countryside transitioning from winter to spring. Behind the drab browns were budding greens, and the first deep yellow dots of lesser celandine erupted between the pale yellow of the local primrose. Yorkshire was on the cusp of the cycle of rebirth once more.

As he drove over a patch of uneven terrain, his luggage rattled on the rack behind him. He glanced back to make sure it was still secure before pressing ahead. He could have used one of the gardener's bins to carry the ritual components the staff had collected for him, but then he wouldn't have access to the things packed in the paired coterminous luggage sitting in his beloved 500. It was better to fully unpack his clothing and toiletries and come prepared from the get-go.

There were four categories of summonings: protected, closed, open, and free. Even though it required more will, he preferred protected summonings. As both the summoner and the summoned creature were constrained in magic circles, it was the safest option. When he needed to be able to move freely, he opted for a closed version, where only the summoned creature was contained in a magic circle. It still offered a protective buffer between him and the creature he summoned without inhibiting his own movement.

Free summoning was anathema to him because neither party was constrained nor was there protection for the summoner. They were often performed by religious devotees with faith in some higher power or greater order. While he knew such beings existed, they were usually real bastards. He had only performed free summonings in dire situations, like when he was stuck in a time loop or wandering the endless hills of Avalon.

Today, he was going to perform an open summoning, wherein he would be in a circle but the summoned creature was free to move around. He didn't do this kind often, but he felt it was necessary to entice a faerie to return to the estate where it had once been bound. Without a true name, he couldn't compel it to appear, and at least he would still be protected by a circle.

After surveying the property, he zeroed in on the forty acres of woodland as it was the wildest terrain—at least, that's how it appeared from the saddle of the four-wheeler. He parked the vehicle at its edge because there was no trail wide enough to drive it in. He entered on foot and within a few minutes, he was surrounded by woods so thick, he could no longer see the four-wheeler.

He searched for an appropriate clearing and found an ideal spot. An ash tree had fallen, taking out several more on its way down. It had landed on a pile of stones covered in thick green moss that was barely recognizable as the ruins of an ancient wall. From the fallen tree sprouted several bunches of black, coal-like mushrooms. A young ash no more than a few years old grew beside it, claiming the prized sunlight and nutrient-rich soil. Its eager roots dove into the stone, eroding what was left of the wall. It was a place where nature was reclaiming formerly tamed land, and the cycle of life and death were all playing their part. If there was such a thing as fae feng shui, this location would be at the height of positive flow.

He returned to the four-wheeler for his luggage as well as a pair of thick gloves and a machete. He wanted to use a flat piece of land on the other side of the ruined wall, but a pernicious blackberry bramble had sent new shoots into the area. They had to go if he wanted to ensure an errant bit of wind didn't move the materials he'd use to make his protective circle. The blade was sharp and he made quick work of trimming the canes back. He saved the long pliable ones to incorporate into his circle because their thorns would sympathetically add to the magical protection of his organic warding. The rest he stacked next to the mossy wall.

He opened his luggage and closely examined all the materials from Buttercrambe Hall. The largest and most important was a complete section of a climbing vine. His best guess was a variety of hydrangea, although he wasn't certain about that. Botany was not a discipline that he was well versed in, and it wasn't important what kind of vine it was as long as it was continuous and unbroken down its entire length. He inspected it and found it was, and there was plenty to work with.

He folded a towel into a square and laid it down in the space he'd just cleared, giving him a dry place to sit. He began to braid the vine into a continuous circle with a diameter of his outstretched arms. It was easy to work because the vine was still green, another boon to his summoning. Faeries found living vegetation more inviting and more than likely, it had been freshly harvested from one of the conservatories earlier today. Although this vine was technically dying, it was closer to life than the one in his coterminous luggage back in Detroit, which was more like rope—brown, dried, and treated to remain supple.

With gloved hands, he carefully integrated in the long thorny canes and finished his garland with the boutique of mixed flowers he'd picked up in town on his way back from the post office: roses, carnations, and daises trimmed at the base of the pedicel. They were just long enough to weave between the plaits, effectively pinning them into place.

He pulled out the shortbread cookies prepared by the Leek's chef before closing the luggage. He rolled the tumblers to 1776, 1989, and finally 2001, and his carry-on traded places with its full-sized counterpart. He waded through all the infiltration gear he usually kept in there until he reached his summoning supplies. In one of the small jars in his bag of components, he found a bottle of dried foxglove—a plant particularly favored by the fae. Ideally, he'd have fresh blooms to offer the visiting fae to take back with them to the middle lands, but they didn't bloom until early summer and there wasn't any for sale at the florist. Dried foxglove would at least perfume the air with the faerie version of catnip. He closed the large luggage and swapped it back with the carry-on in case someone stumbled upon him during his summoning. He placed it to one side along with the gloves and machete but kept them in eyeshot.

He situated the garland around the towel and dribbled crumbled shortbread on his wreath. When it became clear he had plenty to cover the entire circumference, he took a bite or two for himself: he always found it hard to resist shortbread. He then made a second pass sprinkling dried foxglove over the crumbled cookies. With the stage set, he took his seat in the center with a small plastic grocery bag that contained the gifts he planned on using as bargaining chips. It was a hodgepodge collection of objects, most of them shiny: newly polished old buttons, pieces of crystal from a defunct chandelier, small

Christmas ornaments, and small pieces of costume jewelry. The prized possession was a small plastic baggie of Leek baby teeth.

That had been a hard-won concession because Marmaduke knew something as trivial as a piece of hair, a nail clipping, or a drop of blood could be used to hex a person. The Leeks had saved and safeguarded their baby teeth for generations to prevent such tampering, and the practice had continued long after that type of magic went out of vogue. Lord Leek had allowed some to leave the vault under certain conditions: only the oldest teeth were taken and they were surrendered as a last resort. Wilson's esteem of him rose a little at his forethought: it would take a very powerful caster to do a blood curse that affected any living Leeks using those teeth. Even though Marmaduke would not recover from the MEMP, the rest of his family might and it was his job to protect them despite his disability. Wilson didn't expect much of the man compared to his formidable mother, but perhaps he would surprise them.

He placed a white handkerchief on the ground in front of him within the circle and displayed his shiny wares. The bag of teeth he kept in the inner pocket of his jacket. He stilled his thoughts and summoned his will. *Think, think, think....* He took a deep breath and started chanting. His melodious voice rose into the empty forest. Each syllable coated his garland and he felt an arcane surge as the circle closed at the end of the first verse. His protective circle was now powered. He was safe.

Carried on his will, he projected his voice into the Magh

Meall during his second verse and the third went even farther, into the Land of Fae itself. From there, more fae could hear the broadcast than just those in the Magh Meall. In his fourth verse, he did the summoner's equivalent of "testing, testing, one, two, three," letting them know there was an impending offer to visit the mortal realms. It wasn't until the fifth verse that he finally named the faerie he was looking for by the only name he knew: Dirt Feather.

Within seconds, the veil between the realms popped like a balloon pierced by a needle, and fluttering before him was a winged maker. They were naturally curious and reportedly good-natured—the faeries that inspired the Grimm story *Die Wichtelmänner*—in English, *The Elves and the Shoemaker*. Like all of its kind, it was about a foot tall with iridescent wings that shimmered even in the gray light of Yorkshire. Its silver refulgent hair was waterfall braided and danced in the wind created by its flapping wings.

It was hard to tell one fae from another, especially the lesser ones. They did not have as much ability to distinguish themselves to human sight with unique features like the grand fae could. Wilson bombastically greeted his new arrival as if it was a member of one of the noble houses to hedge his bets before determining if this winged maker was, in fact, the same one he'd freed two years ago. "Welcome to the world of the mortals, grand fae."

"Great Liberator, I'm so glad you called me!" it cried out

and flew toward him with open arms. Before Wilson could warn it, it impacted his protective circle with an audible thud, not unlike a bird flying into a window pane.

"Dirt Feather, it really is you! Are you all right?" he expressed genuine concern.

The winged maker shook its body and did a loop-de-loop to test its wings. Once it had regained its equilibrium, it scrunched up its pert nose. "I'm fine, and that's not my name. I am called Glimmer Dawn."

"My apologies," Wilson responded with a bow. "It was the only name I knew to catch your attention."

The fae's wings beat excitedly. "Like you would have any problems attracting attention! I have not forgotten you and I had hoped you would remember me. It wasn't that long ago, was it, even for one of your kind?"

Wilson was puzzled by the enthusiastic reception, but it was far better to have a cheerful faerie than a cross one. "No, it has not been long since we last met, even for me."

"But much had happened in between, no?" it said coyly.

Here we go—the play for free information, he thought. "Yes, a lot has happened since we last spoke."

Glimmer Dawn weaved and bobbed around him, waiting for him to say more. Eventually, it couldn't hold its tongue any longer. "You called me here for a reason. Whatever it is, the answer is yes, but in exchange, I want you to free me from my previous promise to you," it quickly added a caveat so it could not be said it gave the human a blank check. It clasped its little lands together and pleaded, "Oh, how I've longed to tell everyone that I too was freed by the Great Liberator."

"You keep calling me that. Why?" Wilson asked suspiciously. The first time, he'd assumed it was because he'd freed it from Buttercrambe Hall, but no other fae would know about that. The winged maker was oathbound to keep secret who and how it had come to be freed from Leek service—that had been a condition of their agreement.

"Because it is how you are known!" it exclaimed. "And I wish everyone to know that Glimmer Dawn is the friend of the Liberator just as the Liberator is the friend of the fae." Its beautiful face suddenly wrenched with worry. "Have I offended somehow?" It paused at the apex of one of its loops and managed to appear supine whilst still airborne. "Please forgive me! I should not have asked for favors first. My knowing you from the before-time has made me arrogant."

"The fae have a name for me? What do you mean by the before-time?" Wilson grilled it while it was in a talkative mood.

The fae's little head popped up although its supplicant posture remained the same. "You do not know?"

Wilson shook his head. "I know I liberated you from your bondage. Stop bowing to me and tell me what's going on," he said with an open frankness that embodied the spirit of the truth held in high regard by faeries.

Glimmer Dawn came to life, unable to believe its luck.

"Not only am I one who was liberated, I am the one who gets to tell the Liberator that he is the Liberator!" Its demeanor became solemn as it made a pronouncement, "You are hailed the Liberator, as you are the one who broke the chains of bondage that held our eternal Princess Alberia. You are known by all fae as a true friend for returning her to us."

He gulped. "I'm known by *all* fae?"

Glimmer Dawn clapped its hands in joy. "And celebrated as a hero! We saw you next to her when she revealed herself to all of Fae and placed her mark upon you. Her hand has touched you and what she has written, none of my kin can ever mistake. You are the Liberator, and will be for forever and always, until the end of all things."

Wilson did not like the sound of that. He relied upon anonymity for security and becoming a fae celebrity was not something he'd signed up for when he'd returned Alberia and Megan Anderson to their respective homes. He remembered Alberia referring to him as "champion" after she spared him exposure to her full radiance, but never "liberator." And she certainly didn't touch him—he could never have forgotten being touched by such infinite beauty.

His mind combed through the recent past, recalling all the times he'd interacted with Leader, visited Chloe and Dot, and been processed by LaSalle. It seemed unlikely that they knew and didn't tell him. The Nimrud hounds came after that case, but Mau had known him beforehand. Surely, she would have said something if she'd seen something…which begged the question: how had everyone missed the mark of Alberia on him?

He filed that away for later processing and focused on the excitable faerie in front of him. In light of this new information, all the incongruities in its behavior made sense: the warmth of its greeting, freely offering its public name, and prostrating itself to a human. Glimmer Dawn didn't have to remain a lowly winged maker if it could make its association to Alberia's liberator known. It would be able to find a powerful fae from one of the royal houses willing to metamorphose it into a grander sort, perhaps even invite it into clan staff—the first step in the long trek of becoming an actual member of the clan. Social mobility was the one thing faeries, fiends, and humans had in common, and the one thing standing in the way of dramatically improving its standing was the pesky promise it had given in exchange for its freedom. There was a huge amount of social cache at stake.

"You want everyone to know I freed you *before* I freed Alberia."

It bowed its little head. "You comprehend all, Great Liberator." For Glimmer Dawn, it was like discovering the world's biggest band *before* they became famous, only vastly more important.

Wilson could only imagine how much it had killed it to be oathbound to silence for all this time. It must be bursting to tell everyone.

Chapter Seventeen

Buttercrambe Hall, Yorkshire, UK
9th of March, 11:17 a.m. (GMT)

"So, what service do you require, Great Liberator?" Glimmer Dawn asked Wilson a second time with more tact and patience.

He considered his advantages and how best to play it. The first step was to establish if the winged maker could help him. "As you may know, the other faeries bound to Buttercrambe Hall have recently been freed," he opened with a free piece of information to show he was acting in good faith.

It triple nodded. While it had initially stung to discover it would have been freed along with the others if it had simply waited, it would not have the opportunities it had now. "I had heard."

"I wish to ask them about what happened at Buttercrambe Hall before they were freed, but I only have the names their captors assigned them. Do you know their public names?"

The winged maker's brow furrowed. "You work on behalf of the Leeks?"

"No. I work for my organization and the Leeks have asked for our help, but they have no power over me," he clearly delineated the relationship. "I'm investigating the means through which their bindings were broken, but I have no interest in returning them to service and I will not share their public names with any of the Leeks. I merely want to ask them questions about what they saw and heard before they returned home."

The faerie paced in the air, weighing the matter. He had been fair in his previous interactions and he seemed to be telling the truth in this, but it was a hard request, nevertheless. "You will release me from my promise if I give you their public names?"

Wilson interpreted that as confirmation that it knew what he sought and began negotiating. "Freedom from our prior agreement is a great boon for you while what I ask is a small thing. Would it not be better for us to keep the old bargain and to strike a new one instead?"

The little fae played it cool. "What did you have in mind?"

"I like my privacy and there are things you witnessed that I do not want known. If you could provide an equitable service for me, I would be willing to allow you to share the fact that I liberated you before Alberia, but you still could not disclose any details about how it was done and the service you provided for your freedom," Wilson spelled out his conditions. Chloe and Dot would kill him if he let it slip that the Nibelung ring Andvaranaut was no longer lost, and he didn't want anyone to know the Salt Mine had bugged Buttercrambe Hall, especially since it was an ongoing operation.

It was clear from the disappointed look on its face that it had hoped to also cash in on being freed by Andvari's ring. "And you would offer this in exchange for the public names of other faeries that had been bound to the Leeks?"

Wilson paused for effect. "No. That still seems too small a task. If I am held in such high regard, there is a chance they will come even if I call using the name their captor gave them. I have a list of over two dozen; I'm sure some of them would respond if only to catch a glimpse of the Great Liberator."

Glimmer Dawn rued the fact it had talked itself out of an easy bargain. The faeries had come to know each other well over the years; it would have been a simple thing to supply their public names, but now it was going to have to do more. "What if I facilitate your summoning? In addition to their names, I know where in Fae they reside. That would allow you to direct your voice to where they will certainly hear you. I cannot guarantee they will come, but I would be willing to vouch for you. All this I can do in exchange for what you offer."

Wilson took his time and looked at the agreement from all angles. The winged maker tried to conceal its inner turmoil while it waited, but the wringing of its wee hands gave it away. It was clear the fae had nothing else to offer and was truly desperate to make a deal. After finding no foreseeable loopholes or unintended consequences, he extended a small portion of his will outside of the circle. "Done."

Glimmer Dawn released a spurt of its will at his: a kind of esoteric handshake. A new oath had been embarked upon and it was ready to start. "Who's first on your list?"

Wilson pulled out the piece of paper on which he'd jotted down the names from the Leek Family Ledger. "Oddment?"

"Morning Dew, resides in Courland on the Windle River," Glimmer Dawn reported faithfully.

He recorded the information and moved on to the next name. "Tatterdemalion?"

"That's Buttercup, also in Courland, but close to the Hearttrees." It tilted its head quizzically. "Are you familiar with Fae?"

"Somewhat," Wilson hedged without lying. He certainly knew more about the Land of the Fae than most practitioners, but he had not studied fae with the same intensity or depth as he had the lands of the fiends.

"But you are only a mortal, yes? Then it is good that I am here." The little faerie landed on a jelly ear mushroom cap poking out from the stump of a long-gone elder tree. It squatted, grabbed its knees with its arms and folded its wings against its back. "If I mention places that are unknown to you, will that stop you from reaching them?"

"It makes it more difficult, but I will still be able to. There is power in a name that attracts other power, even when the destination is not known," Wilson indulged the fae's curiosity before continuing with the next name.

With Glimmer Dawn's help, he made short work of it. Almost all of the Buttercrambe Hall faeries came from Courland, an ancient location of Fae. It was reputed to be the birthplace of the realm and once its gleaming heart that had since fallen on hard times. Now it was a wild place covered in ruins and was home for misfits, loners, and faeries that were not members of even one of the lesser houses. It made sense in hindsight—if John Leek's intent was to capture a bunch of labor in a short time, Courland was a place to find faeries no one important would miss. According to Glimmer Dawn, the faeries from other parts of Fae had been summoned and bound by one of John's predecessors.

With his list complete, Wilson started his mass-summoning, sending his voice out to specific parts of the Land of Fae and calling upon the faeries by name with Glimmer Dawn riding along. He could feel the relative ease of broadcasting his will now that it was linked with a faerie who was making contact with its homeland. To each name on the list, he made his parley request and Glimmer Dawn added its personal postscript.

Because it had not yet completed its service, it could not disclose its connection to Wilson, but it was certain that acting as his intermediary laid the groundwork for the big reveal that was to come. The first few faeries were dubious about returning to any part of the Leek estate, but they were persuaded when the winged maker said the Great Liberator sought audience with them. From there, word spread quickly.

The air around Wilson's protective circle burst with life as faeries of all sorts popped into the mortal realm. A cacophony of pipes, squeaks, whistles, and toots echoed from all sides as they asked Glimmer Dawn what this was all about. The winged maker fielded their questions demurely like the belle of the ball whose dance card was filling up.

When the final faerie arrived, Glimmer Dawn felt its tongue loosen—it had fulfilled its service! It puffed out its chest, fluttered high. and called the cadre of fae once bound to the Leeks to attention. "The Great Liberator has turned to the one he'd freed from service before he freed Princess Alberia to help bring all of you together."

There was a palpable change as the announcement sunk in. Were they not in the presence of Alberia's Liberator, they would have swarmed, Glimmer Dawn for details—they had always wondered about the details of what had happened when it disappeared from the estate. Instead, they dropped to the ground and pressed their foreheads against the damp foliage. "Liberator, we hail you," they spoke as one. It was one of the unsettling things fae could do when they wanted. They were communicating on some level he couldn't perceive, like how flocks of starlings or schools of fish could move in unison.

"Thank you for answering my call," he greeted them en masse. "I would like to ask you about who was moving around Buttercrambe Hall the day all of you were freed. I believe one of them killed Cordelia Leek and placed the device that broke your bindings and sent you back to Fae. I offer these treasures for your cooperation," he said, spreading his hands wide to showcase the shiny things on the handkerchief.

"Ask, Liberator, and we shall assist without the need of payment," they responded in unison once more.

Okay, maybe being fae famous isn't all bad, he thought to himself. "That is most generous of you. Please rise so we may speak more as equals."

Unaccustomed to such respect from someone so lofty, the faeries were slow to comply but they did in time. They crowded in front of him so that they could bask in the glow of Alberia's mark, which was crystal clear in their fae vision: a glimmering emerald diadem resembling a tree upon which ruby vines pulsated and writhed. It was as fascinating and welcome as a crackling fire at the end of a very long and very cold day.

"You were freed two days ago in my time—the day of the Dawn Club annual meeting," Wilson oriented them in time and place. The time stream in the Magh Meall and Land of Fae did not necessarily flow at the same rate as the mortal realm, and he had no idea how much time had passed for them. "Did any of you see who shot Cordelia Leek in her room?" A sea of heads shook in the negative.

Glimmer Dawn offered an explanation. "We were not allowed to enter Lady Leek's quarters while she was inside, Liberator."

"I see. Did you see someone enter or leave her room shortly

before you returned to Fae?"

"I saw Taylor come and go," a pixie offered, "but Lady Leek was still alive. I could hear her send him away through the door." They might not have been able to enter, but they could still hear through the door.

Wilson pegged that sighting to his timeline. "Marmaduke came in after him. Did anyone see who entered or left her room after Taylor but before Marmaduke?"

They spoke amongst themselves in a rapid-fire communication that was beyond his comprehension. Eventually, the chatter settled down and a tiny faerie no larger than Wilson's pinky came forward. "This is Digger, the one called Rat Catcher by the Leeks," Glimmer Dawn introduced the rat rider. "Go on, tell the Liberator what you saw," it encouraged the shy faerie.

"There was a man walking around the Hall around that time," it peeped out in the upper limit of the human register. "He wasn't one of the family, staff, or a regular visitor to the Hall." The others nodded and backed the rat rider's observation. Some of them had also seen the stranger.

"Could you describe him to me?"

"He was very ugly," the tiny fae answered. Behind him, the others who had seen him vocally agreed.

"Was there anything particularly ugly about him? Was there anything notable about his face or body?" Fae found humans universally ugly and getting them to describe people accurately was not an easy task. It was like playing Guess Who without a board. The faeries chattered among themselves and came to the consensus that the human was just "normal ugly."

"Did this man have the same color of skin as I do?" he obliquely asked about race.

"Yes, like the moon," Digger added.

"And he was definitely a man like me, not a woman?" he checked. He wanted to nail down the gender since the concept could also be nebulous among lesser fae, who were unable to assume one.

All of them nodded their heads. "Definitely not a female— he had hair on his face," the rat rider squeaked.

"What color was the hair?"

"Dark like oak with some pale birch."

Brown with gray, Wilson translated. "Was he an older man?"

Digger hesitated before saying, "I'm not sure." Age meant different things to fae and the course of the human development seemed ridiculous to them. An adult could look the same in as many years as it took a baby to become an adult. "Older than Lady Leek's son, maybe?"

"What about his clothes?" Wilson changed tactic. "What was he wearing?"

The rat rider immediately answered, "He was dressed in black and he wore a hat. That was black too, stiff and at an angle."

The first image that popped into his head was a constable. Unlike American police officers who wore blue across the board, some English law enforcement had black uniforms including hats. He would have thought the staff would have remembered a police officer at the Hall before Cordelia's death, but he also knew how effective a uniform could be at hiding in plain sight. Considering how many cops were there after Cordelia's body was discovered, it would be easy for them to assign the early spotting to that latter time. The brain had a habit of reorganizing memory to make sense, especially if it had some magical help. Being dressed as a constable would give the perpetrator free range to clean up afterward, maybe even EMP the security system and walk out with the incriminating CD. He fished out his phone and pulled up a stock photo. "Like this?"

The faeries elbowed each other to get a closer look at the screen but none tried to displace Digger, their designated speaker. "No, the hat was more slopey—one of the outdoor hats." He was amused at how his brain had parsed the fae's words. Their ability to speak with intent didn't have a dictionary or grammar—it was about conveying meaning and slopey was what exactly what the rat rider meant.

His mind went to someone on the lawn, maybe a member of the lesser families that hadn't been to Buttercrambe Hall before. It made sense to wear a hat at a garden party. He followed up with an image search for gentlemen's hats. One by one, the faeries discounted then all. He racked his brain to come up with other kinds of stiff, black, slopey, outdoor hats. Then an idea came to him—the first person wearing a hat who had greeted him to the Hall. He typed in a different search and showed them one more picture. "Is this the hat?"

Digger's multifaceted eyes softly reflected in the dismal Yorkshire light as it took a closer look. "Yes, that's it!" it exclaimed. The whole crowd relaxed as one mystery was solved. None of them wanted to disappoint the Liberator.

"For future reference, it's called a chauffeur's hat," he informed them. "This man wearing the chauffeur's hat, did he look like any of these people?" He scrolled through the faces of known male SES agents the Mine had sent him, pausing on each one to let them get a good look before moving onto the next. They stomached the parade of grotesqueries quite well, having spent far more time amongst humans than most faeries. When it became too much, all they had to do was glance at the Liberator's forehead. None would be so audacious to call him ugly anymore, but they would uniformly say with confidence that Alberia's mark was his best feature.

He put his phone away after they ruled out the final photo. While he'd hoped for a positive identification, it was a relief to know it wasn't one of the known SES operatives. It would have made future cooperation with the burgeoning agency… complicated. "To sum up your observations, this man was a stranger—someone none of you had ever seen before—who wore a chauffeur's hat. He had dark hair and a beard with some gray in it—probably older than Marmaduke—but he wasn't any of the specific men I showed you."

Among the nodding heads and affirmative noises, Wilson spotted a winged maker that was quite a bit smaller than Glimmer Dawn who seemed less certain on the consensus. He recognized it as Wall Minder, but he didn't want to address it by that name so he consulted his list. "Rowan Bloom, do you have something to add?"

It blushed as all eyes turned to it like a student who had been called on by the teacher. It gathered its courage and spoke, "I think I have seen him before. Once," it qualified. The statement caused a minor uproar as others quickly chastised it for not speaking up sooner—now the Liberator was going to think badly of them as a whole. With a raise of his hand, Wilson shushed them and bid the little winged maker to speak further. "He didn't have the hair on his face then, and there was no birch in his oak, but his eyes were the same."

"What about his eyes do you remember?"

"They were almost not ugly," it said bluntly. "Cornflower with flecks of dandelion before it goes to seed."

"How long ago was this?"

The faerie unfurled its wings and flew two feet into the air. "When Millie was this tall." She had once been its friend when she was very little. It would play with her when no one was looking and she would babble and laugh at its antics. Then, like all human children, she grew out of it.

It wasn't a hard date, but it lined up with the age of the trigger note's stationery, considering Millicent Leek was now a teenager. "Do you remember why he was at the Hall?"

"He had business with Lady Leek."

"Do you know what kind of business?" Wilson pressed.

Rowan Bloom shook its tiny head. "They went in one of the rooms we cannot listen into, even through the door."

Wilson narrowed it down to a handful of rooms that had been warded against eavesdropping once the door was shut. Glimmer Dawn had placed a bug in each location and the magic did not stop them from working—they had produced the bulk of useful information about the family's business and Dawn Club's operation. He smiled at the little one and picked out a shiny button from his handkerchief. "You have been most helpful, Rowan Bloom. Take this token of thanks without obligation."

The winged maker lowered itself. "You are too kind, Liberator." As it took possession of the button that covered half of its torso, Wilson released his summons and the winged maker returned to its part of Courland with its prize.

"Thank you all for coming. I can imagine how unpleasant coming back must have been after your long captivity. I know you do not require payment, but I would like to gift each of you something for your effort." Wilson called each of them by their public name, beginning with those who'd been in service longest. To them, he gave the most desirous items in his hoard: chandelier crystals. Because they refracted light, they created colorful illumination wherever they were hung. Next came Digger, who could barely wrap its hands around a slim Christmas ornament fashioned into an icicle, followed by the many faeries of Courland.

He repeated the same litany with each—a gift with no obligation—before cutting the metaphysical string that brought them here. Eventually, it was just him and Glimmer Dawn. "I suppose you won't be a winged maker for much longer."

"No, but I will always be Glimmer Dawn, friend of the Liberator," the faerie replied, touched by how kind the human had been to his former colleagues.

Wilson held out an earring whose segments were fashioned to look like a fern leaf in repose. "Then take this without obligation so I may know that it is you if we ever meet again."

"Until next time, Great Liberator," it said before bowing deeply and accepting the gift. The winged maker blinked out of existence as he severed the last magical connection to the Land of Fae by way of the middle lands. The faeries were gone and all that was left of their visit was the tiniest footprints in the damp grass and foliage. He cut the power to his protective circle and reeled his will back into his body with renewed purpose. He finally had a lead.

Chapter Eighteen

Buttercrambe Hall, Yorkshire, UK
9th of March, 12:52 p.m. (GMT)

Marmaduke Leek sunk into a plump Chesterfield and stared up at the lime-washed and plastered wooden pendants hanging from the ceiling. The day had started with bad news: his ability to practice the arts would almost certainly never return. It made all the responsibilities that were now his seem heavier. The crime scene cleaners had finally arrived midmorning, and the crew to install the new security system would be here tomorrow. This afternoon, he had to discuss funeral arrangements for his mother, and then there was the meeting with her lawyers.

The will would not be read until after the funeral. Even after her death, Cordelia wanted her family to have a public show of united strength before the private bickering began behind closed doors. Everyone knew he was going to inherit the bulk of the estate, but there was some question about lesser bequeathments. Other members of the family had started cornering him to find out what he knew, and to petition his consideration in case she had left them nothing of substance.

Anyone looking for him would go to his office, which was

exactly why he was hiding out in the Grand Chamber. It was reserved for entertaining, and with everyone doing their own thing, it was blissfully empty. The only person who knew he was here was Taylor, and he remained the soul of discretion. His mobile phone buzzed on the Edwardian scalloped side table beside his chair, and he cursed the necessity of being constantly available. When he saw it was an American number, he relaxed. It was only the Salt Mine agent.

"Hello?" he answered the call.

"It's Wilson. I've finished the summoning and I have a lead. I'll need to speak to whoever organizes the chauffeurs."

"That would be Danvers," Marmaduke supplied the appropriate member of staff from its long roster. "Do you think one of the chauffeurs did this?"

"Probably not, but someone wearing a chauffeur's hat inside the Hall was most likely involved."

Marmaduke harrumphed. "Then it wasn't one of our drivers. They know better than to wear their hats indoors."

"It's possible it was one of the guest's drivers or someone was just wearing the hat to try to blend in. I figured speaking with Danvers would be a good place to start. Perhaps he hired extra help to handle the increased traffic?"

"I suppose it could be one of the Dartlingers..." Marmaduke conceded.

"Dartlingers?" Wilson asked.

"Yes, Dartling Chauffeur Service. We use them during the

annual meeting. There's no way our normal staff could handle the flow. Danvers was quite busy organizing them as they are unaccustomed to how we do things. Did I not mention them before?"

Wilson closed his eyes and held his tongue until the worst of the anger passed. "No, but that would have been helpful to know earlier."

Marmaduke brushed something invisible off his sleeve. "An unfortunate omission on my part. I'll have Taylor send word to Danvers that you'd like to speak to him. When should he be expecting you?"

"Within half an hour," Wilson replied and hung up. Once he was certain the call had ended, he let loose a single expletive, crowned Lord Leek the Upper Class Twit of the Year, and sent the company's name to the Mine. "Did I forget to mention a possible angle of ingress where a stranger could easily infiltrate the grounds and get away unnoticed?" Wilson muttered under his breath with plenty of sarcasm slathered over an exaggerated posh accent, "What an unfortunate omission. Please, do investigate. Pip pip and what ho and all that." He calmed his anger by securing everything on the four-wheeler's back rack and made a beeline toward Buttercrambe Hall's motor pool.

The long garage stretched a good quarter mile along the servants' entrance. The thirteen-car garage constituted one side of the parking lot where staff regularly parked. Wilson's rental was nowhere in sight and he assumed it was parked somewhere in the garage. A series of row houses backed into the parking lot and the other two sides were open to the fields. He drove the four-wheeler into the well-maintained gravel lot: nary a weed or blade of grass in sight. The noise of the four wheeler's engine brought out a figure from an open garage bay on the far end. A man dressed in navy blue coveralls with several old grease stains waved Wilson in. He wiped his hands on a clean rag while he waited.

Wilson noted the two CCTV cameras which hung on large lampposts on his way in. Unfortunately, they were part of the Hall's system that had been fried and any footage they'd captured on the day was on the missing CD. He pulled to one side so as to not block the door and cut the engine. "I'm looking for Justin Danvers."

"The very same," he said with a curt nod. "And you must be the bloke from America. Marmaduke said you had some questions for me?"

His tone was to the point but not impolite. According to the Mine analysts, Danvers had spent ten years in the Forward Repair Team in the Logistic Company of the Royal Marines before becoming head of the Leeks motor pool. He was tall and muscular without being overly so, and Wilson appreciated his quiet air of competency honed by continual trial. This was a man who had work to do, and Wilson got straight to the point. "I wanted to ask you about any recent hires, the Dartling Chauffeur Service, and the standard protocol for parking during the big party."

"Best come inside," Danvers invited him out of the wind and cold. Through the bay door was a fully functioning repair shop. An older model Rolls-Royce Phantom was high on the lift with a single mechanic toiling beneath it. He walked while he talked. "I haven't hired anyone new in over a year. The Leeks would rather staff lean and farm out for special events. We've used Dartling ever since I've been here and I got the name from the guy before me."

And anyone who knew that would know what their uniform looked like, Wilson thought to himself. "Do you perform background checks on them?"

"I do on my guys—make sure their insurance and driver's licenses are in order—but Dartling is supposed to take care of that for their drivers," he replied and opened the door to a glass-paned office with a desk, computer, and small space heater. Wilson judged the clutter as that caused by activity, not laziness, and Danvers removed the debris on the chair opposite his and motioned for Wilson to take a seat. It was tidy enough for a mechanic's office, but Wilson was glad he wasn't wearing a suit. "Like I said, I hired them because the guy before me used them, and they have never given me cause to find someone else."

"Tell me about how things work during big events on your end."

"Guests drive to the house. If they are staying overnight,

their luggage is handed over to the house staff to be deposited in their room. One of our drivers then takes the keys and parks the vehicle back here. The garage is reserved for the family's vehicles and important guests. The staff continues to park in the lot and we park the other guests' cars there as well. When it's full, we start using the overflow lot across the street," he delineated the order of operations.

Wilson gave him a quizzical look. "There are only fields across the street."

"You can't see it from here, but there's a long graveled shoulder off the main road," Danvers explained.

"Did you see anyone acting suspiciously the day of? Someone milling around or someone that didn't seem to belong?"

"No, but I wasn't exactly keeping tabs. With all those cars and people going back and forth, I was just trying to keep everything running smoothly."

"Do you remember an older driver with a beard, brown hair with gray in it, and blue eyes?" Wilson gave him the description he'd gotten from the faeries.

Danvers shrugged negatively. "If there was, he didn't stand out to me."

"Do you keep a list of license plates of all the cars that came in and out?"

"No, but we have cameras installed. You could pull those off the security footage at the house," Danvers said in a bid to helpful.

If only, Wilson rued, noting that he didn't know about the EMP. That was to be expected. It wasn't the type of information that would be spread around. "Can you give me your contact at Dartling?"

Danvers jiggled the mouse. "Sure, just give me an email address." They waited in silence until Wilson's phone dinged message received. "Is there anything else I can do for you?"

"Any chance you could return the four-wheeler to the groundskeeper and have my luggage taken back to my room? I'd like to walk back to the house and take a look at the overflow lot for myself."

Not much to see, but suit yourself, Danvers thought to himself but said, "Sure, no problem." On his way out of the open bay door, Wilson heard him yell for someone called Rodney to take care of the four-wheeler parked outside.

He crunched across the parking lot and passed the row houses occupied by staff with families; only single servants were allowed to live in Buttercrambe Hall proper. It seemed odd to Wilson to live where you worked in this day and age. It seemed to belong to another era with work houses and company towns, but he couldn't find any faults in a pedestrian commute, and given the price of housing these days, perhaps it worked out in the worker's favor.

He walked to the stone wall that demarcated the lawn from the graveled shoulder beside the road. It was empty now, but it could easily accommodate another dozen cars. If it were him, he would have parked here dressed as a Dartling employee and simply walked to the house. It was on the country road that outlined the Leek estate and there wouldn't be any other CCTV for miles except the security system he had to take out anyway.

He pulled out his saltcaster and pantomimed a vape break. When the salt failed to pick up a magical residue, he shuffled his feet along the rocks to disperse the enchantment, although he was pretty sure rain would dissolve it before anyone was any the wiser. A shower never seemed too far away, and the clouds were reclaiming the sky after a brief, sunny respite. He crossed the street to walk back on the sidewalk.

The pavement ran in front of the row houses, leaving a wide strip of lawn between the road and the residences. Wilson ascended the gentle slope that rose about five feet every third front door. His feet found the repeated cluster of steps childishly pleasing, like jumping rope or playing hop scotch. He ducked under the extended eaves to take shelter from the light drizzle and his eye caught something reflective in the corner between the thick wooden brace and the soffit. Someone had mounted a small camera there.

He recognized it as a commercially available starlight-enabled mini-wedge, able to distinguish color at night. It was pretty high-end kit; someone must have had a good reason for installing it. He studied the angle and tried to extrapolate its field of vision: if it was still in operation, it might have captured who left the party early because they knew a MEMP was about to go off. He knocked on the closest door but no one responded. *Of course, no one's home,* he scolded himself. *They're at work and any kids are at school.* He made note of the house number and hurried back to the main house to find Taylor. He would know who lived at number twelve.

Despite using an umbrella, the lower half of his pants were thoroughly soaked by the wet wind by the time he reached Buttercrambe Hall. While he changed into dry clothes, Taylor arranged for him to speak with Lauren Baker, age thirty-six, one of the cooks who resided at 12 Servant's Way with her wife Sandra Clemons, age thirty-four, the resident pantry chef, and her two children, Amelia, age seventeen, and David, age fourteen, from a previous marriage. The couple had worked at Buttercrambe Hall for three years and six months with no demerits on their service records.

Wilson's stomach growled as he went downstairs, reminding his brain that he'd skipped lunch in the course of his investigation. He wound his way through a maze of hallways and countless side rooms until he found the kitchen. It was quite spacious, built in the time when there would be dozens of staff that needed daily feeding. Remodeled many times over in its history, it now had all the modern appliances a cook had come to rely on in lieu of manual labor.

Standing at the cutting board, Baker was chopping her way

through dinner prep when he entered her domain. Her long brunette hair was securely tied back and she wore a white chef's coat, plain black slacks, and comfortable shoes. She stopped mid-onion when she spotted him. "Ah, Mr. Wilson, have a seat." She motioned to the large table in the center of the room where countless generations of servants had taken their tea and meals. "I'll be with you in a second. Care for a cup of tea?" she asked as she washed her hands in the sink and filled the kettle.

"Yes please, and any leftovers from lunch if you have them. It smells delicious."

She ladled him a generous bowl of stew with bread and butter on the side while she waited for the water to boil. Wilson dug in with the gusto all cooks like to see and he was nearly finished by the time the tea was done steeping. She took a seat opposite him with two cups in her hands. "Now, what is it you want to ask me about?" He'd interviewed her yesterday, and she wasn't sure what more she could contribute to his investigation.

"I was walking by the row houses and saw a camera mounted just under the eaves. Is that yours?"

Her face turned grim as she nodded. "Ah, yes. My daughter was seeing one of the village locals. It didn't work out but he wouldn't leave her alone after she broke it off with him. Things went from bad to worse, and I put that camera up so we'd have proof. Landed him a protective order that he found difficult to follow, resulting in three months in the nick. Thankfully, we haven't heard from him since, but we keep it up just in case."

"How do you access the footage?"

She pulled out her mobile phone from a deep pocket and swiped until she found the icon she was looking for. "I use the app that came with the camera—you can see what's happening in real time or review past video. It keeps two weeks of footage backed up on the cloud and you can save and download the part you're interested in onto your computer for longer storage." She showed him the picture on her screen: the sidewalk in front of the row houses, the servant's driveway, and the overflow lot in the wide-range lens of the Dahua camera.

"Do you think you can give me access?"

"Give me a second…bear with…" she solicited for time as she tapped a series of buttons in the settings menu. She knew there was a way to do it because she'd had to set it up on Sandra's phone too. "There! If you give me an e-mail address, I can create a separate user account that can access the camera."

Wilson gave her the same email as he'd given Danvers— one that both he and the Salt Mine analysts could access. He didn't like downloading third party apps, but needs must and his phone had the security Harold Weber and Hans Lundqvist had developed for agents in the field, so there shouldn't be a problem. He smiled once it was installed and opened without incident. "I appreciate your help. If you wait until tomorrow to delete the account, I should have plenty of time to download all the video I need."

"Sounds good. I hope you find what you're looking for,"

she wished him luck as she took his dishes to the sink.

He stole away to a secluded part of the Hall and tucked into the camera feed. Because he could narrow the date and time of his search, it didn't take long for him to find a man dressed as a Darling Chauffeur walking away from the house, getting into a car parked in the overflow lot, and driving away. From there, he merely had to rewind to see when the same man had arrived at Buttercrambe Hall. Once he had those two times, he sent an urgent message to the Salt Mine analysts to download the video and see what information they could ascertain using their top end equipment and enhancement software.

With the request made, he replayed the footage again even though it was hard to make out details on his phone. The mystery man had broad shoulders and narrow hips, and by comparing footage of himself walking up the sidewalk earlier today, Wilson guessed his height at 6'2" or so. Unfortunately, the camera only caught the bottom of his face because he kept his hat on and head down the whole time. He didn't even get a glimpse of those cornflower blue eyes that caught Rowan Bloom's attention. *Definitely a professional.*

There was something familiar about his gait and Wilson couldn't shake the feeling he'd come across him before, but the particulars escaped him. For about an hour he replayed it over and over, hoping to see something new he'd previously missed that would give him a clue to the man's identity. On his umpteenth viewing, his phone dinged: the analysts *had* found something. The car was a new Vauxhall Astra. While the stone wall was just tall enough to obscure its license plate and the camera was at the wrong angle to capture it on its way in and out, they were able to find it via nearby traffic cameras. Wilson wolfishly smiled. With a license plate number, it was only a matter of time. If they were lucky, they might also catch a face.

Chapter Nineteen

The Magh Meall
Summer Epoch

The sun was well above the horizon when the Ivan Dmitrivich Rasputin awoke. He had no sense of where he was or how long he'd slumbered, only that he was still in Baba Yaga's mortar and Yhtill was perched beside him. The boy had been up for some time, patiently watching him sleep with all seven eyes. He perked up when he saw the object of his observation was finally awake.

"You are human," the boy stated, reaching out to lightly touch the Siberian's nose with the tip of his diminutive finger. Then, he touched his own nose with the same finger and giggled. "I am human too, but I have more eyes than you do. I see all the things. That's what Baba tells me. She says I see the things she sees."

Rasputin, still a little groggy, didn't know how to properly respond, so he said nothing, which Yhtill took as an invitation to say more. He prattled on in the fugue way that children did, telling stories before understanding narrative structure. "I see that you were born when the trenches and fields of Europe were filled with mustard gas. That your mother was a whore whose nose rotted away because of syphilis. And once, you poked the eyes out of a cat and put it in a room of an empty house to see if it could find the mouse you blinded that you'd put in there earlier." Rasputin's mouth went dry. He didn't know how the child knew these things, but he hadn't felt a trace of magic used against him.

Yhtill smiled. "That is the once-was times I see. Would you like to know what I see in your will-be times?"

"Leave him alone, Yhtill," Baba Yaga gently scolded at the helm of the mortar. "He shouldn't know what comes. That is only for us to know."

His three pairs of eyes blinked and looked up at her innocently. "Sorry, Baba," he sweetly apologized, but his seventh eye never stopped staring at the Siberian, who shivered under its gaze.

Rasputin took to his feet to avoid looking at it any longer and scanned the scenery racing beneath them. It was still tree-covered but the typography was a long mass of rolling mountain folds oriented northeast by southwest instead of the flat terrain. Small clearings dotted the endless forest where holy places in the mortal realm had created areas in the Magh Meall that trees avoided.

"We are nearly there," Baba Yaga informed him and pointed at a ridge that was indistinguishable from the others. She whispered something to the mortar and the spell that had protected Rasputin from the cold lifted. The chill was still unpleasant, but the air was noticeably warmer than had been that in Russia. The mortar descended in a smooth gyre to just above the treetops where it carefully navigated through the leafy deciduous branches until it eventually settled upon the forest floor with a soft bump that belied its weight.

"Out," Baba Yaga ordered. "He who you seek lies on the other side of the veil. Return when you are ready but make haste. We will not wait forever." With a big smile, Yhtill nodded several times behind her. As Rasputin scrambled out of the mortar, the hag already had a breast out to feed her hungry son. Yhtill's paired eyes gloated as he latched on.

"I will be as quick as I can, great Baba Yaga. If it is not quick enough, I want to thank you for your assistance in this matter."

Baba Yaga pushed the massive pestle in Rasputin's direction and shunted him out of the Magh Meall and back into the human world. His abrupt arrival scared away a nearby animal and the noise of its scurrying caused the insects to temporarily silence their umbral song—they were no longer alone. It was dark, but the night here was not known to him. The stars were all wrong and the air smelled different.

He surveyed his surroundings and found himself standing before an old, run-down house built on a small piece of precious flat land amongst forested hills. The yard had long since reverted to wild, growing weeds and tall grasses like an imported patch of untouched prairie. The numerous saplings—

two of which were growing through the rusted-out husks of old automobiles—suggested it was only a matter of time before it returned to the forest that surrounded it. As run-down as it looked, it reeked of magic. Given its look and age—not more than a hundred years' old—he guessed he was somewhere in the new world.

He focused his will and created a small bobbing bit of light about the strength of five candles. It floated in front of him, and he directed its path through the armpit-high grass to the rickety wooden stairs that led to a long, wrap-around front porch. He held his hand up to the closed door and felt two different wards pulsing with power on the other side: fear and apathy. It was a traditional pairing used to keep out non-practitioners. Anyone who touched the door would be struck by an overwhelming sense of dread about what lay beyond, followed by a sense of deep apathy to kill any curiosity that might outweigh the fear. Their subconscious would fill in the gaps and come up with reasons why they didn't want to enter.

Rasputin carefully walked along the porch, making sure to step on the joists instead of relying on the integrity of the decking, which had already failed in a few places. As he went, he found the interior sill of each window and the back door similarly warded as the front door, but he didn't detect any alarms. It didn't make any sense to him—why place and maintain wards to keep casual passersby at bay but not protect it from magicians who would have little problem pushing past fear and apathy wards? It made him suspect he was missing something. He circled the entire house one more time but didn't find anything else besides fear and apathy. He dared not spend more time searching, lest Baba Yaga leave him stranded in a strange and distant land.

Because the back porch was smaller and in much better shape, he pushed his way in there. The interior was as derelict as the exterior and his nose immediately detected the scent of nesting animals whose small raisin-sized droppings littered the floor. He did a sweep of the first floor and found nothing of interest other than a wall calendar from 1981 hanging in the kitchen. It was printed by a septic system repair company based out of Moorefield, West Virginia. He was not familiar with the name, but it was written in English and sounded American to him.

He hazarded the rickety stairs to the second floor and entered each room until he found what he was looking for: a linen-wrapped body surrounded by a large pool of dry putrefaction. He checked for magical protections, but only found a series of wards inscribed on the baseboards to keep animals from entering the room. He pushed his ball of light into the room and entered.

The once-white linen had been stained with the dark reds and blacks of decomposition, but it did not interfere with the sigils of non-detection that had been painted on. While they were visible to the naked eye, it rendered the bundle invisible to arcane vision. It explained why he could never discern Yanchik's location—whoever had placed him here slathered the entire shroud with a thick coating of anti-scrying magic. The only break in the sigils was over the forehead of the skull where the Latin phrase, *requiescat in pace*, was painted. It was repeated in Russian over the nose and mouth.

As soon as he read the Cyrillic, he pulled at the layers of the linen. When he found them stitched together, he withdrew the small knife he always carried with him and ripped at the seam. The body had completely decomposed and he caressed what was left with his will but there was nothing useful left. Whoever had wrapped it had pre-emptively put the soul to rest, which explained why his attempts to speak to his Yanchik on the other side had also failed.

His eyes watered with regret now that he knew for certain. He folded the linen back over itself and allowed himself a moment of grief before leaving the house with his son. At least he knew the truth: there was nothing of Ian Lancaster left to plan, assist, or execute the assassination of an Ivory Tower chairman, which meant someone else knew his magic and had used it to incriminate a dead man.

A niggling thought broke through the pain: *why take measures to hide it from my arcane sight but do nothing to physically secure it?* Perhaps someone wanted him to find the body to give him a proper burial? Someone who wanted to let the Siberian know his son had been killed at the hands of someone who used Russian to magically hide it from his sight?

Was this a message? Had the Ivory Tower murdered his Yanchik? If that were the case, why would Major General Yastrzhembsky ask for his assistance? Had that been a double bluff? And why hide the body here? Were they trying to implicate the Americans?

The Siberian frowned at his spiraling thoughts: he did not like spies and their games. He knew he was no good at playing them nor did he want to be. Cradling the linen-wrapped bones in his arms, he extended his will into the night, hoping Baba Yaga was still there.

Chapter Twenty

Over the Atlantic Ocean
11th of March, 4:05 p.m. (GMT-3)

Surprisingly, Wilson found himself crossing the Atlantic in hot pursuit of the MEMP bomber. The UK license plate had led to a car rental agency which, with a little bit of magical nudging on his part, produced a name: Charles Nathanial Rice. He'd hoped for a copy of Rice's photo ID—a normal requirement when renting a vehicle—but they only had a passport number on file, not a scan. While the rental company couldn't explain the breach in protocol, Wilson suspected he had not been the only one to use a little enchantment on them. He begrudgingly gave this Rice fellow credit where it was due.

Contrary to popular media, criminals weren't masterminds. They were just people, and people were dumb and sloppy on the whole. Practitioners were just people with the ability to interact with magic, and even with that benefit, there were usually multiple paths that led to the culprit. This one, however, had been very careful and crafty, and Wilson had had to adjust his game accordingly.

When he'd submitted the name to the Mine, he figured it would be this case's choke point: the bit of information that would jump-start a stalled investigation once discovered. What he hadn't counted on was how much ruckus it would create. It turned out that Rice was a non-person, a figment of the CIA. It was an alias that only existed in a customizable Singaporean passport in a Malaysian safe house. Wilson had had cause to use such identification in the past: they scanned like legit passports and operatives simply had to insert their picture to use them.

It set off red flags in the system because Rice had been one of four such passports stolen from a CIA safe house in Melaka City, along with the gold kept alongside them in the hidden stash. After Kanali Patel—Salt Mine codename Prism—had reported the break-in and theft, the CIA conducted a regional audit and found two more safe houses had been looted of their gold: one in Bangkok and the other in Manila. Whoever had hit them knew to disable the hidden cameras and, far more damning, knew of their locations at all—a closely guarded secret in the agency.

This led Wilson to profile Rice as a professional with a funding issue, one with the discipline to only take the passports he needed. They were intended to be used and burned, not sold for capital. It was possible to move passports for profit, but it required proper criminal connections which increased one's exposure. Gold, on the other hand, was ubiquitous—easily and discreetly turned into cash with minimal effort across the globe. It also suggested Rice was either CIA—or had been—or the agency had a leak. Neither of those options sat well stateside.

Wilson had hoped to keep his investigation on the down-low in case the SES was tangentially involved, but that was impossible once the CIA wanted answers. The upside was assistance from UK border control. Although there were no records of Charles Rice entering the UK, he *had* left on a plane bound for San Jose, Costa Rica, the morning after the MEMP. With CIA backing, the Mine's analysts had requested airport video through official channels because hacking into Heathrow International's security was an entirely different affair than hacking into the UK traffic camera system. They hadn't managed to get usable facial images from the traffic cams, but they should get better images from Heathrow, something that they *could* run through facial recognition.

After some back and forth, the agency had reluctantly released the names and nationalities of the other three stolen passports. From there, the Mine's analysts were able to construct a timeline of their target's movements. One had been used to gain entry into Moscow four months ago. Another had been used to enter London the day before the MEMP. Rice's leaving made three. The fourth passport had not appeared in any airline passenger manifests in the last six months. Wilson assumed the last one was to help him flee Costa Rica. It looked like his operation was coming to a close.

The mere mention of Moscow made Wilson think of the Ivory Tower. It would be a prime target if Rice was going after magical agencies, but surely they would have contacted the

Salt Mine if someone had set off an MEMP in their territory. There had been a well-established precedent of interagency cooperation between the Mine and the Tower when it came to forbidden magic.

He supposed Cordelia's death and the strike against Dawn Club leadership could have been an Ivory Tower mission, but that didn't make sense with the connection to the compromised CIA safe houses. Nation-state agencies didn't need to steal petty stashes of gold to fund operations, and there weren't triads operating in Malaysia, Thailand, and the Philippines around the time of the thefts—he'd already had the analysts check.

He supposed it could be an operative within the Tower doing work on the side who didn't want their bosses tracking their movements, thus the necessity of the CIA passports, but he was pretty sure if someone in the Ivory Tower had hit those safe houses, they would have taken everything they could to liquidate, especially if they were already coloring outside the lines. Who'd care if it took them another six months to get rid of the passports? They were good money just waiting to be grabbed.

As much as he hated to admit it, a rogue actor within the CIA needing capital for a private affair sat best with Wilson. Perhaps those unaccounted for months in Russia were the target working in cahoots with someone in the Ivory Tower? Anything was possible.

The question that had really stumped him was: Why San

Jose? It wasn't a hub of anything economic, political, magical, or what have you. It was possible this was Rice's getaway and he was saving the last passport as a reserve get-out-of-jail-free card, but Wilson had had the analysts dig for links between Costa Rica and either the Dawn Club or Ivory Tower, just in case.

That's how he'd come upon Arthur Wilton Sleeker-Stanley, age forty-four. Wilson recognized the family name from the Leek's guest list, but Arthur had not been in attendance. He had fled the UK six years ago while on bond after being charged for multiple rapes, including of minors. Rather than face trial, he'd resettled in San Jose. Since then, the UK government had been trying to convince the Costa Rican one to expatriate him, but they had not complied with the request. Wilson was pretty sure the decision to relocate the Sleeker-Stanley's shipping business to Costa Rica mere weeks after Arthur had arrived played a role in that.

The Mine could find no other connections between the Dawn Club and San Jose, so they had forwarded him the entire file they'd created on Sleeker-Stanley. It made for grim reading. One of his victims was a thirteen-year-old girl trafficked from Slovenia and she was far from the only one. It was enough to make Wilson consider breaking his rule about no alcohol while on a case. When the flight attendant offered him final beverage service before the plane landed at Juan Santamaría International Airport in two hours, he chose tomato juice instead and continued reading. He was three days behind Rice, and if he was being honest, he wouldn't be too sad if he caught up with him *after* he'd taken out Sleeker-Stanley.

Chapter Twenty-One

San Jose, Costa Rica
11th of March, 7:05 p.m. (GMT-6)

Once he had but one name given to him by his mother and father. It was the only name he had needed for twenty-five years, but there came a time when he was given another which he'd borne even longer—for most of his life, really. But now, he had a new name, the first that was not assigned to him: Vithar. The original Vithar was the son of Odin, an Aesir god who'd avenged his father's death by ripping apart the giant maw of Fenrir at Ragnarök, and one of the few that survived the apocalypse to see the birth of the new world. He didn't normally lean toward such grandiosity, but it felt like such a good fit that he'd humored himself. He was on a mission of vengeance and through it, he would find a new world.

He was a big man with large hands and broad shoulders, but not muscle-bound like the action heroes of film and television. While he was tough enough to get the job done, it was a clandestine strength—more like a Dick Butkus than a Jack Reacher. He found it easier to blend in this way, even in Costa Rica where his tan was still too fair to pass as native.

He was just another old *gringo*, and the locals were just glad he knew Spanish, albeit with one of the Mexican accents.

The sun had gone down over an hour ago, and he was bunkered in a hole hidden among the raucous tropical foliage, staring into the backyard of Arthur Wilton Sleeker-Stanley. His back was against a fallen log, the stump of which shielded his body from view. He still didn't like the look of the two security cameras that covered the back of the property and the alleyway behind it—he still didn't know if they had night vision or infrared capabilities. They hadn't been enough to put him off, but they had made him dig in like an Alabama tick. He used the copious vegetation at hand to break up his heat signature to appear non-human if anyone was checking the cameras' feeds to be on the safe side. It was an extremely unlikely event, but unlikely didn't mean never.

He had done the bulk of his scouting last night, but he felt it prudent to take one last look to make sure nothing had changed before he committed. He closed his eyes and quietly took deep breaths, making each inhalation progressively longer than the previous exhalation. Using pranayama meditation, he lowered his heart rate and allowed his blood to hyper-oxygenize from his over-breathing. After he took the deepest inhale he could manage, he forced additional air into his lungs with muscle contractions similar to those used in swallowing. Free divers called it lung packing and as he did it, he looked a bit like a fish out of water, repeatedly opening and closing its mouth.

Once his lungs were full to bursting, he separated his spirit from his body. Before he ventured away from his physical form, he confirmed his antahkarana was connected to his belly button. In the past, it had anchored him to the mortal realm during jaunts to the Magh Meall, but now, it tethered his spirit to his body as he wandered about the Land of Dead. He did not welcome the thought of being trapped there.

He flew through the soft edge just on the other side of the human realm. The cold didn't bother him because part of him was dead inside, and the part that didn't belong here—his body—wasn't trying to come in. He followed the path his corporeal self would have to take and cleared the rooms and passages in his ghostly form. When he found the house was as it had been yesterday, he returned to his body and shivered upon re-entry. His breathing and heart rate returned to normal as he acclimatized to being whole again.

He put on a pair of thin leather gloves and gathered his things. It was his second time in his hole, but it was also his last. He rested his paintball gun on the stump in front of him and took out both of the security cameras, double-tapping their lenses to make sure he'd gotten them. Had he more time and resources, he could have done something more elegant, but sometimes a primitive bypass was the best option. It wasn't like there was a team of guards ready to respond; he'd pegged the system as a passive one and he just had to make sure it didn't capture his part in Sleeker-Stanley's death when its feed was accessed later.

He secured the paintball gun in his backpack and hustled down the hillside. He crossed the alley and went up and over the eight-foot-high wall in the one place they'd failed to put enough glass on top to prevent a determined climber. The extensive backyard featured a large pool with a separate jetted lane for swimming against a current. There were deck chairs and a pool house beside it, and an English herb garden that was quite a departure from the lush native tropical plants. A concrete path hugged the wall, connecting the three-car garage to the house.

Vithar kept to the concrete without worry of being seen. All the cameras pointed outward: he'd seen none inside the property on his reconnaissance. Considering it was Sleeker-Stanley's own personal security video evidence that had damned him back in the UK, it made sense he didn't want another record of what happened in his new abode.

The lock on the sliding door was pathetic; it fell to a simple rake attack on the second try. He opened and closed it behind him, making almost no noise in the process. In the distance, he could hear the muffled sound of the BBC news on the television. That would be his target in the media room opposite the Romanesque courtyard around which the house had been built. He drew his pistol—an IWI Jericho 941 that he'd boosted from a lone Costa Rican police officer—and removed from his pocket one of the pumice stones he'd purchased from a beauty and healthcare store after his first reconnoiter. The first was for Sleeker-Stanley, and the second was for the sylph his target had summoned to protect him after he'd caught wind of the MEMP from his family back in the UK.

Sylphs were air elementals most commonly used as guards. They killed by sucking the air out of a victim's lungs while pinning them on the ground with a weight that felt like an elephant's foot. Vithar had seen the results of their work; it was an ugly way to go. Although animals could often sense them, they were invisible to the human eye. He'd only spotted it while he was ghostwalking. On the other side, his senses weren't bound to conventional rules.

He trod carefully on the tiled floor but picked up the pace once he was on the carpet. The sylph could not sense him while he was in the Land of the Dead, but it was only a matter of time before it perceived an intruder was inside. He made a break for the master bedroom—as far away from the entertainment room as he could get while still being in the house. If he didn't make it before the sylph discovered him, things could get tricky real fast.

He breathed a sigh of relief when he made it and left the door open behind him. He stood in the far corner facing the hallway, bracing himself for a fight, and it didn't take long. An invisible force tackled him like a defensive lineman. He collapsed hard against the floor but the carpet absorbed most of the noise of his landing. With the wind knocked out of him, his monkey mind wanted to panic but he kept a cool head. It was impossible to escape the weight pressing on his torso, but his limbs were free. He brought the pumice stone in his hand to his mouth, forcing the elemental to make contact with it if it wanted to continue to suck the air out of his lungs.

As soon as the rock bridged the gap between human and elemental, the sylph was banished out of the mortal world. It was an old, powerful sympathetic magic: pumice was composed of countless tiny little chambers of air encased by rock and now, somewhere in the elemental plane of earth, the sylph was trapped like all those pockets of air in his pumice stone. It would eventually erode its way out and return to its native plane of air, but the crucial point to Vithar was that it wasn't here crushing him.

Pumice, not just for making your heels smooth, he joked as he put the stone back in his pocket. He hadn't seen a second sylph, but caution was king.

He took a second to catch his breath before creeping through the house to the media room. On a massive television mounted on the far wall, a BBC news presenter was discussing the current train wreck in the Middle East. In front of the screen was a leather sofa and recliner, in which his target sat. Vithar kept to the wall, keeping distance between him and the man as he edged his way to the front of the room. As with his previous targets, he wanted Sleeker-Stanley to see him before he died, to understand it wouldn't have ended this way if he'd made better decisions in the past. Despite this desire, his Jericho 941 never wavered from the recliner; he'd shoot earlier if he had to.

Sleeker-Stanley turned his head when he caught movement in his peripheral vision but said nothing. He silently and smugly grinned at the intruder for almost half a minute until it dawned on him that the sylph wasn't coming. That's when the panic set in. "Who are you? What do you want?"

Vithar's head tilted to one side. "Wow, you really don't remember me, do you? I know it's been a while, but I haven't changed that much. Maybe you'd remember better if I were a thirteen-year-old girl." Sleeker-Stanley started to summon his will but before he could do anything with it, Vithar fired two bullets center mass, followed by a head shot for good measure. Once he was certain Sleeker-Stanley was no longer among the living, he exited the premises the same way he'd entered.

He trekked through the hilly jungle, warm and still even at night. He didn't travel quickly in the dark as the way was rough, and by the time he crossed the greenbelt and got back to his rental car, he was drenched in sweat. He drove back to his hotel with the windows down, preferring the wind of a fast car over the air-conditioning when he was soaked. He was ready for a long, cool shower—ready for a baptism of sorts. The last of the bastards directly responsible for his betrayal were now taken care of and he had one clean passport left. He hoped it would be enough to get him where he wanted to go.

The air-conditioned hotel lobby seemed downright chilly, but he welcomed it having significantly dried of during the drive. When he got to his room, he casually tossed his backpack onto the floor of the closet adjacent to the entrance and made a beeline to the toilet. There was nothing worse than needing to hit the head when you're driving, especially on bumpy roads. He tucked and flushed and was just about to turn on the shower when a voice behind him spoke.

"Put your hands on your head and turn around slowly."

He couldn't help but grin, both at his own rookie mistake of not securing the area when he'd first entered and at the familiar voice. He was a big believer in kismet and it only seemed right that it was *him*. "Easy sport, don't shoot, I'm complying," he said as he slowly raised his arms and turned around.

It only took Wilson a split second to recognize him. "You!"

Chapter Twenty-Two

San Jose, Costa Rica
11th of March, 10:23 p.m. (GMT-6)

Wilson rarely found himself speechless, and   Edward Kane—codename Patron—gave him time to get over the shock. While Wilson may have had no words, his Glock never wavered. His first thought was that Kane had been alive in deep cover—like Stigma—the whole time, which was a fine theory except he had been present at his death. It was part of the reason he hated Lukin so much. It had been the Russian's bullets that had put Kane down years ago during that dreadful night in Singapore. He hadn't been able to stay on the scene for long because the police were already on their way, but there was no surviving that head wound. Even after all these years, he sometimes saw it in his dreams.

This next thought was that it wasn't Kane at all, but someone or something assuming his likeness. There were a number of supernatural creatures that could mimic appearance, not to mention magicians with a talent for illusions. During his first year in training, he and Kane had code phrases to confirm their identities to each other in the field because the unity-of-being ritual had yet to be perfected when Wilson first started at the Mine. Even if they were dealing with something that could steal memories as part of the subterfuge, it was unlikely those would be taken. To a mimic or memory thief, they were trivial compared to the bigger memories that composed the concept of self for a person.

"What's the phrase?" Wilson asked curtly.

Kane smiled that big grin of his. "Oklahoma sucks." As a bona fide Texan, it brought him a deep sense of joy to say it out loud. "And yours?" he asked in kind. Whenever one asked for the phrase, it was required for the other to give theirs to prove they were themselves.

"Idaho, Canada, Nevada," Wilson answered. "Okay, let's say I believe you. Now tell me how that's possible."

"It's kind of a long story, one I'd rather not tell standing in a bathroom with my hands on my head."

Wilson reached over to the door and flipped the deadbolt and swing bar to prevent Kane—or whoever was doing a pretty good Kane impersonation—from doing a runner out of the hotel room. Then he backed into the main room to make sure he was out of lunging distance; Kane was almost a foot taller than him. "Okay, you can come out. Over there," He motioned to the chair in the corner. He kept his gun pointed at center mass as the older man lowered his arms and took a seat.

"You've gotten older—lot more salt in that pepper than I remember," Kane observed.

"Funny, you haven't aged a day," Wilson replied. It had been eight years since Singapore, and he found it suspicious that Kane did not look any older.

"Clean living and a sense of purpose can do wonders for a man," Kane said drily.

"Cut the crap," Wilson swiped at his bait.

"Still haven't developed a sense of humor, I see. I'd thought you be happy to see me?"

"I will once you explain how you're here."

Kane silently harrumphed at Wilson being Wilson. "Fine, be that way. I don't know what Leader told you when she sent you out after me, but I was supposed to be working with the Dawn Club to hunt down use of time magic. At least, that's what they told Leader and it looks like she believed them. Turns out, I was really helping the Dawn Club and the 88th Bureau retrieve an object that had been stolen from the Chinese. A potion."

"What kind of potion?"

Kane leaned forward in his chair and answered evasively, "A very important one to the 88th. To make a long story short, during the mission I found out why the 88th wanted the potion and that the Dawn Club had, at the very beginning of the mission, contracted with the Ivory Tower to kill me once the operation was over."

Wilson held up his story to how he remembered their last encounter and it seemed to fit. When he'd arrived in Singapore,

Kane had not been his normal self, and he hadn't found a shred of evidence pointing to time magic, either. "So that's why you looked so cagey when we met…you were waiting for the other shoe to drop."

"Yep. I was biding my time, hoping to find an opportunity for us to slip away from our Dawn Club handler to notify Leader, but I must have tipped him off somehow. He knew I knew and must have called in Lukin early."

The oddities in Lukin's behavior that had bugged Wilson for years were suddenly making sense: he had been improvising. Instead of his usual MO, he'd openly attacked Kane in public, guns blazing like a 1930's Chicago gangster. Rather than covering his tracks, he had fled the scene almost before the last shot had been fired, hiding his appearance with layers of glamours. He was only there to kill Kane and must have not expected Wilson to be there. It also explained why afterward, the Dawn Club had been—to borrow a phrase from Kane—as useful as tits on a bull.

Despite all these revelations that seemed to fall into place, Wilson noted Kane had not said anything substantive about the potion. "What was so important about this potion?" he asked again.

Kane shook his head. "No can do. That's a Leader-level question, but I can tell you that she'll want to know what I know." There was an implicit challenge in his slightly taunting tone that was both familiar and infuriating to Wilson.

"Well, I'm the one with the gun," Wilson pointed out. "And so far, you haven't told me anything that a good conman couldn't conjure up."

Kane leaned back and his voice turned rugged like a piece of old leather. "That doesn't change my answer. You're either going to kill me or not. Either way, I'm not going to break my word. Ask me another question."

Wilson was slightly annoyed at how apt a response it was. Kane was old-school—a man was only as good as his word. Of course, anyone who'd profiled Kane would know that about him, but there was something genuine about the way he said *break my word*. It sounded like he meant it.

There were still a lot of questions to be asked so he started with the big one. "How did you survive?"

"You were there. You saw what happened. I didn't. I died. That's the God's honest truth."

Wilson squinted suspiciously but played along. Hadn't he arguably "died" a few times since joining the Mine? "Then what happened?"

"Last year on the 20th of October, I woke up in the bathroom stall of a restaurant half a block away from Hong Lim Park in Singapore minus those pesky bullet wounds. My first instinct was to report in, but when I found out eight years had passed, I held off."

"What about the potion?" Wilson chimed in.

Kane shrugged. "It had waited for eight years. It could wait a little longer. I had bigger things on my mind: How did I come back? Did someone do it to me and, if so, who? Why?" To almost anyone else, it might seem inconsistent to risk getting shot to keep the nature of the potion secret while also not immediately reaching out to Leader about what it was, but it made sense to Wilson, and he knew it would have made sense to Kane. "So, I decided to go to ground until I had a better handle on things. I snuck across the border to Malaysia—"

"And hit the CIA safe house in Melaka City and then Bangkok and Manila," Wilson interrupted. It was one thing he didn't miss about Kane: how long the man could take making a long story short.

Kane smiled—Wilson always was a quick one. "Well, Manila then Bangkok, but that's just splitting hairs."

"How'd you know where they were?" Wilson wondered. He only knew the ones he'd visited personally and to his knowledge, Kane hadn't done extensive field work in Southeast Asia.

"Did you ever meet Catherine Charmaine—cute blonde with long legs—CIA admin out of D.C.?"

Wilson thought for a second. "Sounds familiar, but I can't really place her."

"We had a fling. Nice enough lady, but she wasn't the best with security…I eventually had to report her. She'd once left a list of safe houses lying around and I memorized most of it. I thought the information might save my butt someday and I was right. Anyway, after Malaysia, I did a little digging about what's changed since I've been gone—man, has the world gone to shit!—and I decided payback was in order. After all, I was long dead and the bastards would never see it coming. There would never be a better time. I hit the other two safe houses to make sure I had enough funding, now that I had a goal."

"So, you just appeared in a bathroom stall like nothing had happened?" Wilson backed up. "Did you feel any different?"

"Well, I've never been dead and come back before, so I'm not sure what it's supposed feel like. I'm not a revenant or vengeful spirit, if that's what you're asking," Kane reassured him while glossing over his full situation. There were things he didn't want Wilson to know until he had a chance to talk to Leader about them. Then, he had an idea to prove to Wilson he was telling the truth. "When I woke up, I had all the belongings on me that I had when I was shot. Here, let me show you my wallet as proof."

Wilson nodded and Kane slowly reached into his pocket so as not to startle him. He still had a gun pointing at him, and although Wilson was a cautious and deliberate agent, there was a twitchy part of the little guy that you didn't want to pluck at. He tossed it far enough for Wilson to keep his distance while picking it up. It was a battered tri-fold crocodile monstrosity with a Lone Star tooled on the lower right corner of the worn exterior: the wallet Kane had always carried. It was a dead match to the one Wilson had in one of his safes back at the 500. He'd managed to get it off Kane's body before fleeing the scene to make it harder for the Singaporean police to identify him. He wasn't a sentimental man, but he'd been glad that Leader had let him keep it.

"Looks right," He tossed it back and Kane put it away in his front left pocket. Wilson was coming around to this being the real Kane. Not many would know the make and material of his wallet, and since he had taken it from the scene, it couldn't have been duplicated afterward.

Kane noted Wilson's slight change in body language and exhaled ruefully. "So, the wallet is what convinces you and not me."

"I'm not convinced yet, but I'm struggling to think why anyone would make such an ugly thing twice."

Kane was pleased at a hint of humor that was creeping into their conversation and hazarded a question. "Okay, my turn. How'd you find me?"

"License plate number on your rental in the UK."

"Bullshit! There weren't any cameras that I didn't take out."

"One of the workers' homes had a small private camera. It was well concealed and fortuitously placed. We only got a partial face on you as you walked toward the Hall, but it was enough to figure out the make and model of the car you drove to Buttercrambe Hall. From there, it was only a matter of checking traffic cameras on routes. The whole thing rolled up after that."

Kane grunted. "It's always the thing you miss that makes you. How'd you find my hotel room?"

"Once we had the names of the stolen CIA passports, I had them brute-force it—called all the local hotels checking for any of the names. Had your hotel and room number by the time I landed. Meanwhile, Heathrow still hadn't sent the video from you boarding your flight out," Wilson groused. "I decided to come here because I still didn't know if I was facing a single enemy or part of a Tower triad. I'd thought about setting a trap at the Sleeker-Stanley house, but…"

"If you don't know what you're hunting, you're the prey," Kane finished the sentence. It was one of the first things he'd taught Wilson. It was impossible to create a proper trap for an unknown opponent, particularly in their line of business. "No need to worry about Sleeker-Stanley."

Wilson nodded. He'd more than half expected as such. "I can't say I'm sorry for coming too late," Wilson admitted.

Kane nodded. "I had to rush a bit on him. I'd saved him for last because I knew he'd be the easiest of the three."

Wilson tilted his head. "Three? Who's the third?"

Kane did the math and picked out clues from Wilson's account. When he put it together, he practically burst at the seams. "You don't know? You really don't know?"

"Know what?"

Kane giggled like a child and slapped his knee. "Looks like that slippery sucker kept it under wraps, after all!"

"Are you going to tell me or just gloat?"

"Alexander Petrovich Lukin—Sasha to his friends, if he had any—is dead."

"You killed Lukin?" Wilson sputtered.

"Bastard put a couple of bullets in me, only seems fair I got to do the same."

"But he's the chairman of the Ivory Tower?!" Wilson objected.

Kane kept giggling. "I know, right? Who'd have thought that turd would ever get to such a position? I took a long time planning it, but let's not kid ourselves: the reason why the high-ups don't get taken out is the threat of retaliation, not an inability to reach them. When the cost of taking a leader out is all-out war, no one makes the order to take a leader out."

"And you did it anyway?" Wilson asked incredulously. His brain was spinning off all the varieties of fallout that were surely on the way and the assassination alert he'd gotten before he'd even left for England. "This is bad…real bad. We have to get out of here. The Tower is going to hunt you down."

"Simmer down, sport. I did a severance ceremony on him. There's no more Lukin to Luke about anymore. He's *all* gone and there's no way the Tower can unravel how it happened without Chloe and Dot's help."

Wilson and Kane had been the ones who'd permanently settled the Goshawk problem. Chloe and Dot had done the lion's share of the work deciphering the severance ceremony—

he and Kane had gone over it countless times without figuring it out—but once they had, tracking down Lancaster had been easy. Leader had taken care of the body and to the rest of the world, he'd simply gone off the radar. "You Goshawked Lukin?"

He grinned another wide one. "The Russians will never stop chasing their tails on it."

Wilson couldn't contain a short laugh at Kane's deviousness and he stopped once he realized what his brain had done. He wanted to believe it was Kane, but he also didn't want to die because he wanted to believe. For a moment the two men sat quietly, each lost in their own thoughts.

Eventually, Kane broke the silence, "Sorry I missed your thirteenth. I would have brought a six-pack of Donettes to the party."

While Kane was referring to the traditional Salt Mine party that happened on an agent's thirteenth anniversary, Wilson dialed in on the Donettes. "What kind?" he asked deliberately, keeping his voice even and void of interest.

Kane looked upward and rubbed his chin. "Well, I believe someone once said, 'There can be only one Donette, and that one is chocolate!'"

Wilson holstered his weapon. "Why didn't you lead with that?" The only other person that knew chocolate-covered Donettes were his guilty food pleasure was Stigma. When Kane had found out he had, for some reason, rode him on it so much that he hadn't shared it with anyone else.

Kane barked a laugh. "Where's the fun in that?" He looked around at the tired hotel room, just one of thousands he'd stayed in. After months on his own, it felt nice to be in familiar company again. "You wanna to get some food? The nearby *sodas* has some kickass *pollo frito*."

Epilogue

Leader sat in her fourth-floor subterranean office reading the latest news from Russia. Lukin's death had just been made public—a helicopter accident that also claimed the lives of Colonel Anatoly Durov, a member of the Ivory Tower's Interior Council, and the pilot, an airman unaffiliated with the Tower. Yastrzhembsky must have pinned Lukin's murder on Durov—it was the only way the rest of the council would sign off on taking out one of their own. As long as he had enough damning *kompromat* on any doubters, they would go along with the narrative. Durov had always been a bellicose voice in the council, and in a nest of vipers, one makes friends or gets bitten.

According to Fulbrecan, there was chaos once more in the Tower elite, and how that would shake out could not be accurately predicted. She hoped Yastrzhembsky did not try to assume chairmanship. She didn't want to go head to head against him, and not just for sentimental reasons. He could be a transformational force in the Tower if he wanted to be. Keeping the chairman's death under wraps for nine days and orchestrating the elimination of a rival in a method that justified the closed-casket funeral Lukin's mangled corpse required? That was something that took skill, finesse, and imagination. Her preference for Ivory Tower chairmen was a series of barely-to-mildly competent people, because an incompetent one could be almost as dangerous as an excellent one.

And then there was the matter of the Siberian. Unbeknownst to him, thirty minutes after he had left the derelict house that held the remains of Ian Lancaster, a small motion-detecting, pin-hole camera set into one of the old electric outlets had relayed a video of his time spent in the main bedroom to a powerful transmitter secreted away in the attic. The transmitter had then blasted the video to a rarely used email address that automatically forwarded it to a second address and then to a third one before it finally arrived in Leader's digital pile of incoming messages via a direct forward from David LaSalle. She hoped he would follow the false leads she'd planted back to the Tower, but she couldn't be certain he would.

That was the beauty of suspicion. It didn't have to be foolproof to erode trust; a whisper was all that was needed to fan the flames of speculation. She wondered if this would stop him from helping them in the future. After all, the Siberian was not beholden to the Ivory Tower and Yastrzhembsky would be a fool to challenge him directly. Even she would avoid a direct confrontation with Rasputin, not so much because of his ability—he was still a youngling and she was confident that she could best him—but because of his association with Baba Yaga.

She had not considered he would turn to her to find Lancaster and was even more surprised the eld hag had carried him from Russia to the New World to retrieve the body, but the video confirmed what her imp spy had reported via Bentback. A magician of the Siberian's caliber would not call upon such an old power lightly, and Baba Yaga was not who you called when you needed a ride. As hard as she found it to believe, it appeared the hag had some sort of actual *affection* toward the Siberian. She would have liked to find out more about that relationship, but Fulbrecan had no leverage on Bentback and there was no pretense for them to safely communicate on a regular basis, especially now if the Siberian suspected the Ivory Tower had a hand in Lancaster's death. It was one of those rare cases where she'd outsmarted herself. Oh well.

She returned to Lukin's public obituary even though that was not the reason she was at the office on a Sunday. After Fulcrum tracked down Patron in Costa Rica, the Mine had a lot of work to do to cover up the trail they had just ferreted out. Then there was the matter of getting Patron out of Costa Rica without using a passport he'd taken from the CIA safe house. And that was just the beginning of damage control. He had made a right mess of the delicate balance of power.

While she was annoyed with Patron, she couldn't say it was out of character. He had always been one to ask forgiveness rather than permission. If he'd come in right away, she wouldn't have sanctioned any of the murders and would never have approved the use of an MEMP. He did it his way so that responsibility for those decisions was his alone, and she just had to decide what to do with him. She couldn't decide if it was selfishness or a misplaced sense of chivalry—quite possibly both.

"Enter," she replied to the crisp knock at the door.

LaSalle cracked open the thick door and made his report. "We've finished processing Patron—it's definitely him and he's another Child of Tesla." It came as no surprise. It was far too coincidental that Patron had been reborn so close to the time Deacon had acquired the Tesla coil from the stage magician Ward the Magnificent, brother of Cameron Carver, the Mine's latest provisional field operative-in-training.

"Has he been instructed on how to bind his spirit to his body?" she asked as a matter of course. Binding the spirit to the body had become the modus operandi whenever they came across a person brought back to life by Tesla's coil. Without such action, the spirit was merely possessing its own body, leaving it open to exorcism as well as some metaphysical erosion of the barrier between the mortal realm and the Land of the Dead.

LaSalle's face broke into a rare enigmatic smile. "We didn't need to. He's made his own arrangement. He can separate his spirit from his body, travel around in the Land of the Dead, and return by using his antahkarana."

Silence filled the office as she took it in and submitted a

new piece of information into the mental ledger where she did her sums. "How remarkable," she said dryly. "Where is he now?"

"Being held in a room in the gauntlet," LaSalle answered in brief. Even if his spirit left his body, it wouldn't be able to travel far with the runes and sigils in place. "He says he's ready to be debriefed on his last mission, if you'll see him."

Leader sighed. "Better send him in." If she was going to pin the MEMP on Sleeker-Stanley, she'd need as much detail as possible.

THE END

The agents of The Salt Mine will return in *Going Under*

Printed in Great Britain
by Amazon

44088807R20115